FEMINIZED AND PRETTY 2

Emasculated and cuckolded by a dominant wife

(Femdom and Transgender)

Lady Alexa

Copyright © Lady Alexa 2023

All rights reserved. No reproduction, copy or transmission of this publication or section in this publication may be reproduced copied or transmitted without written permission of the author.

This novel is a work of fiction. Names, characters, businesses, places, events and incidents are either the products of the author's imagination or used in a fictitious manner. Any resemblance to actual persons, living or dead, or actual events is purely coincidental.

Contains explicit scenes of a sexual nature including male to female gender transformation, female domination, CFNM, spanking and reluctant feminisation. All characters in this story are aged 18 and over.

Strictly for adults aged 18 and over.

Dear Reader,

I hope you enjoy the second novel in my three-part series of forced feminised, 'Feminized and Pretty'.

If you enjoy reading about feminisation and female domination, then subscribe to my Newsletter to receive exclusive forced-feminisation and femdom stories, additional chapters from my books and free serialised stories not available elsewhere.

Go to ladyalexauk.com to subscribe to my FLR & Feminisation blog and Newsletter

CONTENTS

Chapter 1 – That schoolgirl look

Chapter 2 – Recollections of a male life

Chapter 3 – Walk like a girl

Chapter 4 – Feminised and pretty hairstyle

Chapter 5 – The office affair

Chapter 6 – Feminised and pretty naked

Chapter 7 – Maid time

Chapter 8 – Dinner party

Chapter 9 – Feminised and cuckolded

Chapter 10 – Go to your room

Chapter 11 – Morning glory reflections

Chapter 12 - The Mistress plan

Chapter 13 - Mistress is pleased

Chapter 14 - The new journey begins

Chapter 15 – Girl training

Chapter 16 – Introductions

Chapter 17 - Taken behind

Chapter 18 – And there's more

Chapter 19 – Feminised and pretty sore

Chapter 20 – Mistress rules

Chapter 21 – The men will adore you

Chapter 1 – That schoolgirl look

Elizabeth loved to see her husband wearing a schoolgirl's skirt. He looked so damn cute and submissive.

Every few seconds her eyes flicked from the road to the grey box-pleated skirt laying across his thighs. The sheer stockings on his smooth legs reflected an amber glow from the street lights. Her hands were gripped with concentration on the steering wheel as they crept slowly in evening rush hour traffic.

Patrick stared down at the floor in abject humiliation. His long straight hair hung across his cheeks. He didn't care for the broad smile of satisfaction slashed across his wife's face. He had never seen Elizabeth so pleased. She was struggling to contain her amusement; she snorted out sniggers every few minutes.

They were on their way back to her West London home; a home that had become a feminisation prison for him. He'd thought he had escaped in a dash for freedom. Instead, he had fallen into a trap, like a hopeless fly sucked back into

Elizabeth's web of contacts. In this case, Melissa Stone had revealed herself to be another link in his wife's network. Melissa, his aunt, had betrayed him. He headed back to his virtual prison driven by the head warden: his wife.

Before meeting Elizabeth, he'd lived an unrestrained life. And poor, that much was true. His rich wife had given him warmth, good food and humiliation. He had left his small cold apartment forever. He had rarely had enough money for the gas and electricity meters before he met Elizabeth. He was skinny, food was a luxury on what he earned as a musician. At first, he thought he'd won a life lottery by meeting the wealthy successful Elizabeth. Looking back, he had swapped one prison for another.

He punched his thigh in exasperation with a balled fist. A surprised glance shot from Elizabeth's amused face. He had been stupid to think Aunt Melissa would help him escape. He had turned up at her house in the rain in soaking-wet female clothing. Aunt Melissa had claimed to have no male clothing and given him a pleated skirt, white blouse and stockings to wear. How stupid was he to have believed that story? But he had believed her and put them on to stay warm as the only option. Or so he thought. He was still wearing the humiliating schoolgirl outfit and his wife loved it. She wanted him to remain dressed like this.

Whatever the pros and cons of his life now, Elizabeth's giggling was grating on his nerves. She was normally cool and reserved. She had put him in a skirt before; why was she now so amused by his appearance? He smoothed down his skirt without thinking. He pulled his hands away and it caught Elizabeth's attention and she dissolved in more giggles. She was acting like a little girl.

"Elizabeth?" he said.

Elizabeth looked away from the road at him for a short moment and then back. Concentration was etched in her forehead as she manoeuvred around a parked taxi. A group of young women jumped out, ready for an evening of fun. Unlike him.

The traffic was slow and the drivers were impatient. The starless night sky was iron grey and rain spattered against the windscreen. Elizabeth flicked the wipers on.

"Ms Remington," she said, her face locked into concentration.

"What?" he drawled. He rarely understood his wife's replies and motivations these days.

"You will call me, Ms Remington. I've told you before Patricia: Ms Remington." She braked hard as the lights ahead changed to red. He fell forward, locking the seatbelt.

"But you're my wife, what's going down? It's not cool to be so formal."

The engine idled in the stationary traffic. A young man in a battered hatchback made his engine roar behind them; the exhaust growled like a wounded animal.

"Yes, I'm your wife but also your Mistress and owner. And Patricia, I want you to stop with the fake mid-Atlantic talk, your musician days are over. You sound like a bad imitation of an ageing English rock star. You will address me as Ms Remington. I've told you this before. I want you to say it or face the consequences when we get home. I can make you walk home in your little skirt if you prefer?" She put a crooked finger to her lips to stifle another giggle.

Patrick put his head in his hands and then pulled them back through his long hair in exasperation. He leant back in the car seat. "OK. *Ms Remington*." Anger bubbled inside him. "Please, Ms Remington. What do you find so amusing? You've seen me in a skirt before. Shorter than this one."

Elizabeth sniggered, fighting to stop giggling. "It's the genius of Melissa. She made you wear schoolgirl clothes and you didn't realise. I love it. I wish I'd thought of that. And you put the clothes on without argument." She dissolved into hysterical laughter.

The lights changed and she pressed on the accelerator. The car jerked forward and she changed gears between bouts of laughter. The route home was locked in the endless back-to-back traffic, like a slow train of steel and lights. Patrick cringed. Melissa had fooled him.

Elizabeth stopped giggling. "Tomorrow you will go to work dressed as a schoolgirl. I'm going to find some little white socks and tie your hair in two side ponytails with pink bows. I can't wait." She gave up fighting her laughter and fell into a fit of giggles, spurting out, "*Schoolgirl. I love it. Pleated grey skirts, incredible. Melissa is a genius."* She howled with laughter.

Patrick slumped back into the car seat, folded his arms and set his lips tight. He had a bad feeling his life was about to become even more humiliating.

Chapter 2 – Recollections of a male life

As they drove home, Patrick remembered how he used to play his guitar in bars and pubs before meeting his wife. It had been an easy life. He had had little money but little responsibility either.

The girls had loved his cool troubadour persona. They never lasted long. That was not a problem. He never had any money or any initiative to do anything besides practise on his guitar. It hadn't mattered, there was always another girl at his next gig who would catch his eye and his cheeky grin. He'd direct a few silly jokes at her during his gig and he'd be set up for the night. It always worked. Whenever he was down, he'd pick up his guitar to blow away the cares. There was no guitar now.

Then six months ago he'd got a gig at a new place; a smart bar in west London. The manager had warned him not to swear, it was not the kind of clientele he usually played to. That was the night Elizabeth walked into the bar and into his life. She was twenty years older than him. He had watched her come in and hadn't given her any thought. The *rich bitch* comment had floated through his mind though. He had resisted telling her what had been on his mind, remembering the manager's instructions. That would have meant no more gigs at that place. He wasn't going to get any more gigs anywhere anyway.

He had scanned the bar for young girls to pick up that night, the rich bitch was not on his mind. His eye had settled on a mini-skirted woman at the front of the bar. She had been facing him, her short skirt somehow managing to ride up even further once she had spotted his eyes were all over her. The glimpse of her white underwear was deliberate.

During his break, he had sat at the bar sipping a free beer hoping to seal the deal with this young girl. He always managed to cadge a free drink or more with a cheeky quip or a promise. The barman was a young lad with aspirations to play guitar. Patrick had promised to give him a few lessons. All he had to do was top up his glass free of charge. Patrick exaggerated his London accent to sound more bohemian. He called the barman *mate* a few times and dropped his aitches.

Patrick hadn't noticed Elizabeth approaching him, he was too engaged in telling his new *mate* the barman about the exotic life of a musician. All the while he was making faces at the mini-skirted girl.

Elizabeth had tapped him on the shoulder at that moment. She told him she may have something for him and to call her number; she left him her business card. He had thought she may have wanted him to play guitar at a dinner party. She was a striking-looking woman, although almost old enough to be his dear-departed mother.

Elizabeth had left the bar after leaving her card with him. He had told his new friend the barman that Elizabeth was a stuck-up *bird, using* the old-fashioned London slang term for attractive young women. The barman raised his eyes to the ceiling at Patrick using a word that had passed its sell-by date in the previous century.

Once he had called Elizabeth, the beautiful older woman, it was clear she wanted something else. Him. The romance had escalated. At first, he'd thought it was fun to make love to an older woman. He quickly saw her as a way to get a few free drinks, good food and a quick *shag*. *Shag* — another London slang word now forgotten by most other people. He still used it to talk about sexual intercourse.

He assumed he was doing her a favour. He was a much younger attractive and witty man for her to hang on her arm. They saw each other a few times and Elizabeth dazzled him by taking him to smart restaurants and bars. Elizabeth proposed to him after a month. Her proposal shocked him at first but soon saw the opportunity. He decided to use his practised charm to extort a few million pounds out of his new fiancée, soon to become wife. He had suspected that the poor dear Elizabeth was desperate for a toy boy. She bought him new expensive clothes but left his hair long.

What he hadn't realised, until it was too late, was what she had really wanted from him. She wanted a submissive feminised husband as a housewife. She had zeroed in on him as the perfect naive, self-absorbed and ignorant man she had been looking for. With his slim frame and long hair, she saw the perfect raw material. Once she had uncovered his real reasons for marriage, she decided there were to be no boundaries.

"Patty." Elizabeth's booming voice invaded Patrick's memories of how he got into this situation. "If only you had behaved yourself and not tried to take my money then your life would have been much easier."

"How so?" he asked.

"I did want a feminised husband, that much is true. Someone not very intelligent. You fitted the criteria perfectly, Patricia." She chuckled again.

Anger and frustration rumbled inside him.

Her face hardened as she stared into the line of red tail lights seeming to stretch into the horizon. "Your life would have been comfortable living with me. I would have made concessions, not pushed your feminisation so far. You would have lived a pleasant life as a feminised husband. Now the gloves are off. I can do anything I please."

Patrick wondered how much worse this could get. He was about to find out.

Chapter 3 – Walk like a girl

The morning after his return home, Patrick sat in the kitchen, his hands on his lap. He was dressed in a grey box-pleat schoolgirl skirt and a white fitted blouse. Elizabeth had kept her promise. She adored the outfit Melissa had put him in and made him wear it again today.

He didn't have to go to work at her office that morning. His initial relief at this news from Elizabeth was soon shattered: Elizabeth had other plans for him that morning. Then he would go to work in the afternoon. Dressed in the schoolgirl outfit.

Elizabeth had left for work two hours earlier. He was alone with Elizabeth's personal assistant, Clara. Clara had just finished two phone calls to arrange Elizabeth's plans for him.

Clara rubbed her hands together as she told him to put his coat on. She had set up two appointments, the first at a hairdressing salon and the second at a beauty parlour. He had listened to Clara with mounting anguish as she discussed on the phone how Elizabeth wanted his hair dyed and styled. Then he was to have a pedicure and manicure at the parlour. Maybe this was not so bad, he told himself. His nails and his long hair were untidy. Elizabeth had an account at both places and was their best-paying regular customer. Clara gleefully told him they had shifted other customers around to accommodate Elizabeth's request at short notice.

Clara threw Patrick's pink coat to him.

"Hey, Mistress Clara? How are we getting to the high street?" he drawled, hoping she was taking him in the car. The idea of walking along a busy road dressed in a short grey pleated skirt was horrifying.

"On foot, of course. And stop with the fake rock-star language, Patty. You're becoming a pretty girl now, not a male musician. You need to talk like a girl."

His worst fears were realised. His face sunk like a stone dropping through clear water. Clara swished around the kitchen and grabbed door keys, her purse and mobile phone. She swept them into her handbag. Patrick pushed his arms into his pink coat in slow motion as if that would stop the inevitable trip. He was going to have to go out into a busy high street dressed in female clothing. Again. He told himself he'd got away with it on his ill-fated escape to Melissa's; he could do it again. He touched his thigh, silky in the stockings. A lump came to his throat.

Clara went to the front door. She called him towards her with an index finger raised to her eye. He got up from the stool as if mired in treacle. He trotted towards her in his one-inch heels. He hoped that they would look like two girls out together. They were a similar height. If he kept his head down to the ground, he may get away with it. The biggest problem was that Clara was in trousers and he had a short skirt and long exposed legs. That might attract attention towards him.

They left the house and walked in silence for the ten minutes it took to get to the high street. He ambled past other pedestrians, head down, trying to look casual. He peeked up from his lowered head. Most people were going about their own business uninterested in two girls out for a stroll. A couple of glances came from men but they may have been the normal stares of men for attractive women. A quick check at his reflection in shop windows showed that with his head down he looked like a slim female. As long as he kept his head down, maybe no one would notice he was male.

Clara turned into a double-fronted hair salon. He followed her in, pleased to be off the pavement. He kept his head down. No one in the salon looked at them, Elizabeth's attempt at humiliation hadn't worked. She had made him walk along a busy high street in schoolgirl clothing and he had got away with it.

In some ways, it was enjoyable: the unrestricted freedom of a skirt, the air around his legs. He didn't understand why it was that way but he was fine with it. It seemed like a small victory against his wife. She had made him wear an embarrassing skirt and he had not minded. OK, he admitted to himself, he enjoyed it.

Chairs, sinks and mirrors lined both walls beyond a reception desk of reclaimed wood. A young lady in a white jacket and blond straightened hair greeted them with a nod of her head and a practised smile.

"Hair appointment for Patricia Remington. It's on

Elizabeth Remington's account," said Clara. "This is Elizabeth's husband, Patricia," she announced loudly.

Patrick hunched in absolute horror. The receptionist looked up and at him with a start. They locked eyes for what seemed like ages. Her eyes returned to her booking screen, bored. "Go through Clara, Candice will be Patricia's stylist today and she's waiting for you." The blond girl's eyes shot up again to Patrick. They floated over him.

"Why did you do that?" he whispered to Clara from the corner of his mouth as they stood in front of the reception desk. The receptionist's eyes went from Patrick and then to Clara and back to Patrick as if she were watching a tennis match.

Clara's eyes glinted and her mouth twisted into a scheming expression. "It's Mistress Clara. If you question me again I'll put you over my knee, pull your panties down and spank you in front of all these nice ladies."

The receptionist sniggered and then pulled her lips in to stop. Patrick gulped.

The salon buzzed with stylists dipping and moving around their clients. He caught the eye of an attractive girl blow-drying a customer's hair. The stylist wore a green suit with culottes and dark tights. She smiled back at him. Two other stylists worked on a lady's blond hair filled with metallic pieces. One stylist was a male, the other a lady. They were prodding and feeling her hair as if in a series of dance moves.

Patrick pushed his hands deep into the pockets of his pink jacket. The pleated skirt hung below, pressed against his long legs. It was as if he was watching a surreal movie with him as the unwitting star.

Clara took his arm and guided him round to the chair at the end of the row. He felt the glances on him as they made their way. He approached the empty chair and saw who he assumed to be Candice waiting for them. Clara and Candice kissed on each cheek. Candice introduced herself to Patrick. She then kissed him on both cheeks too. If she had realised he was a man, she didn't let on. It was probable that since Elizabeth was such an important customer, they accepted her eccentricity. An eccentricity of having a feminised husband in a pink jacket and miniskirt.

Candice told him to sit down in the chair. Her manner was

brusque and businesslike. It was as if she were trying too hard to pretend the situation was normal. Candice immediately started to buzz around him like a mosquito he couldn't wave away.

Candice's blond hair cascaded over her face and shoulders. Long false lashes batted as she spoke. Her tight red dress rode up her thick thighs. She pulled on the hem with a free hand, wiggling her hips each time she tugged. Her breasts appeared ready to escape from a low-cut front that was low and revealing. Her thong outlined the taut dress. A small roll of fat, like a partially inflated bicycle tyre, ringed her waist. Her perfume wafted around him, invading his throat. She tottered about, heels clipping and clopping on the floor like a dancing pony.

Patrick sat back in the stylist's chair. Clara spoke to Candice by his side. "Elizabeth would like you to dye her hair blond. Very blond. She wants Patty to have a fringe to her eyes and her hair styled in a long feminine bob look."

Patrick looked to Candice who nodded. It seemed as if it were the most natural thing in the world to have a young man in her salon chair dressed in a short skirt about to have a feminine hairstyle. He tried to get up. Clara's hand rested lightly on his shoulder. "Be a good girl, Patricia, and stay where you are."

He sat back at her command. Much of the fight had gone from him. There was nowhere to go, no one to turn to. He closed his eyes and tried to relax. Let them do what they want, he thought. If he fought against them, he would lose. He told himself to accept it. It would be less stressful that way. He preferred no stress. What would he look like with blond hair? Feminized and pretty?

Chapter 4 – Feminised and pretty hairstyle

A dull pain throbbed through his head. He rubbed his temples with the ends of his fingers as he stared in the mirror. His hair was silky and smooth. He had spent most of the morning in the salon with Candice doing his hair.

Candice had stomped around behind him as she finished her work. Her heels tapped on the hard floor as she fiddled and fussed with his new hairstyle. He watched her in the mirror, concentration written on her made-up face. She ran a hand-held hairdryer over his hair and fluffed it up. The warm air and her soft touch soothed his headache.

"What do you think, Patty?" Clara's nasal voice cut into his head. "I love it, it looks very pretty."

He didn't answer but turned his head from one side to the other. His hair moved as one piece like a sail in a light wind. It was beautiful and incredibly feminine. His penis twitched with a flush of excitement. His face broke into a smile and he almost said *wow* before he forced himself into a stern expression. He bit his lips tight. These feelings were wrong and he pushed them away.

Candice had dyed his long hair a shocking golden platinum blonde. Candice had applied straighteners and then curled the end of his hair under. His fringe covered his eyes and also curled under. It rested on his lashes. He blinked and shifted on his chair. He didn't like the feelings he was having. His penis stiffened hard. A small tent appeared beneath the cover Candice had thrown over him. He fought against the erection; he didn't want anyone to see his excitement. He wanted to hate his hairstyle not to love it.

"It's very pretty, Candice." Clara pulled at the sides of his new blond style. "Do you like it, Patricia? It looks like you do." Clara's eyes dropped to the small tent covering his erection. He pushed his hands over to cover his excitement.

"You look cute," Clara said as she opened a plastic bag she was holding. She removed a pair of small white socks. "I popped out to buy these for you. Put them on before we go to get your nails and eyebrows done."

He took the socks from Clara. He rolled them around in his fingers. They were short and brilliant white with a pink frill around the top. He held them up at Clara with a pleading look. Clara raised her eyebrows and nodded slowly and deliberately. He removed his shoes and put the little socks on over the stockings. Resentment burnt in him replacing his initial excitement.

He accepted that Candice was only doing her job for a well-paying customer. Clara though was different, a nobody living in the vicarious power from his wife. Clara enjoyed that power and this ate at him. Defying her meant that he would have to face the wrath of Elizabeth. He was trapped into doing what she told him. He was already in the centre of Elizabeth's sights after his temporary escape to Melissa. He didn't need to give her more ammunition to make his life more hellish.

Clara stood next to Patrick as he put his pink jacket on ready for the short walk to his next appointment. He was a twenty-eight-year-old man in schoolgirl's clothes. He had no make-up on and his male facial features were obvious. The socks had made his clothing more girly, more feminine. His appearance was bound to get looks and maybe comments.

Clara told him to hurry up, they were late. She took his arm and pulled him to the door and out into the busy high street. His teeth locked together in desperation at his imminent humiliation. The nail bar was three shops away. The walk took two minutes. It seemed like two hours. Sniggers and laughter greeted his every step. People pointed at him. Two white-van drivers hooted their horns. His face burned at the ignominy. He didn't believe that walk of shame in the socks had been Elizabeth's idea, that had been Clara.

They entered the nail bar with a flurry as he pushed in as fast as possible to get off the street. A lady in a white coat with a face mask around her neck showed him to a seat in front of a white bench. They seemed not to be surprised by his appearance. Patrick assumed Clara had pre-warned them about his arrival. They had probably got the same story as the employees at Elizabeth's office — the story that he was a transvestite or transgender who wanted to transition to a woman. The ladies there were probably thinking they were helping him.

The lady beautician sitting opposite had large eyes like thin brown almonds. "You're very pretty, my dear. What would you like?"

He hesitated. He didn't want anything there, it was what Elizabeth wanted.

Clara leant on the back of his chair. "She wants long false nails in a bright pink, please Mariel."

Long nails were what he didn't want. He snatched his hands away from the tabletop. He thought that it may be possible to negotiate. Mariel sat back, not wishing to get involved in a looming dispute.

"Why don't I have my toes painted pink but clear on his fingernails? And no long false nail. That would be fair," he suggested, plaintively.

Clara moved around to stand next to Mariel. "This isn't a debate, Patricia, it's about what Elizabeth wanted for you."

He shoved his hands in his jacket pockets. His bottom lip protruded. Time to stand up to Clara's bullying. *Be a man,* he thought. He touched his pleated grey skirt and it chipped at his strength. He didn't know if he could stand firm but he had to try.

Clara's eyes tilted to the ceiling. "Are you going to let Mariel do her work or am I going to have to call Elizabeth to talk to you?"

He thought for a moment. He didn't want long false nails. How would he do anything while hindered by them? He tightened his lips and pushed his hands deeper into his pockets. He had to stand up to Clara. He had acquiesced too easily at the hair salon. Now it was time to make this stop. Clara shoved her mobile phone into his face. The screen said one word: ELIZABETH. The icon was green, the speaker symbol on. She was on the line.

"Patty?" The robotic sound of Elizabeth's distant voice roared from the speaker and into the room.

"Yes, dear?" he said with a nervous catch in his throat. He glared at the screen as if he would see her there.

"Don't you *dear me,* Patricia." She shouted. He imagined her striding around her office, heels banging on the floor, face red with anger.

Clara clasped the phone hard, her red nails locked over the

black case. He shuddered.

Elizabeth's voice boomed from the phone's speaker. "You will call me Ms Remington and you will do everything that Clara tells you."

"But, but she…" he stammered.

"DON'T *BUT ME,* GIRL. GET YOUR NAILS DONE OR I WILL DEAL WITH YOUR INSOLENCE WHEN I GET HOME. I. WANT. YOU. TO. BE. A. GIRL." Her screaming voice blared from the phone speaker. "And a girl you will become."

He heard her gasp in exasperation. The phone went dead, the nail bar was in silence. The beauticians froze in what they were doing, staring at their hands, avoiding eye contact. He passed the phone back to Clara whose face shot an *I told you so* expression. He placed his hands on the table, his shoulders down like a scolded dog.

Mariel opened a rectangular plastic box and began choosing long false nails. Clara pointed at a colour card. Bright shocking pink.

"This afternoon you'll be going back to work at Elizabeth's office. The girls there will be pleased to see how much more feminine you've become."

Patrick closed his eyes and sunk into the chair. Mariel took his fingers and started her work.

Chapter 5 – The office affair

The lift jolted as it stopped. A sense of impending panic came over Patrick on his return to work at his wife's office. He was the most junior employee. Clara stood next to him without speaking. Frosty animosity fizzed between them like the sparks from snapped electricity cables.

The lift doors opened and he swallowed hard. The all-women office had all seen him dressed as a girl before. His new schoolgirl style with blond hair and long pink fingernails was worse. His short white ankle socks with the pink lace tops caught his eye. Black Mary Jane shoes and stockings.

He was thankful that the box-pleated skirt was longer than the skirt he'd had to wear to the office last time. He did not want to walk out of the lift and into the office. He put out his hand to his eyes in disbelief. The nails were twice as long as his natural nails and covered in luminous pink. He rubbed his fingers over his eyebrows. Mariel had thinned and shaped them as two high arches. At least Clara had taken him to the office in the car.

He stepped gingerly out of the lift and into the office. Elizabeth waited, hands on hips. She beckoned him with an index finger. He lumbered to her and stooped, head down. Her eyes ran over him. She lifted one of his hands. "I like your new nails. Do you?"

"No," he said, like a moody child.

"Good," Elizabeth replied. "Now get back to work, Patty, there's a good girl."

He sloped to his assigned desk, feet dragging. Jackie, his young manager, watched as he approached. Her face lit up like a thousand-watt bulb. Patrick had not complained to Elizabeth about the schoolgirl skirt he was wearing. It was humiliating, of course, but longer than the previous skirt Elizabeth had forced him to wear in the office. It was mid-thigh. It was a strange situation when he was pleased to wear a skirt he thought. It was all relative and another small mercy as Elizabeth didn't allow him to wear panties.

He had been unable to stop his erections the last time he had been in the office. The smallest growth in his penis had sent it peeking below the tiny hemline, his humiliation revealed to all. Today the skirt covered his penis. That much was good.

Elizabeth was so engrossed in dressing him as a young schoolgirl, she had missed this worse humiliation. The humiliation of exposure.

He slid into his seat next to Jackie and smoothed his skirt down. He noted it was becoming a natural movement. He would have to be careful not to acquire too many feminine mannerisms. This was proving difficult. The mannerisms were coming naturally. He pushed a strand of hair from his face. Another feminine movement.

Jackie's face darkened. She was unhappy with something. She was usually so pleasant, so easygoing. He racked his mind for a reason. It came to him. He had borrowed her London Travelcard from her drawer to use for his great escape on public transport. It had not been such a great escape. A great trap. The result was that he was now more feminised than before he had escaped. Hair, nails and eyebrows like a girl.

"I'm sorry, Ms Swann," he said to Jackie, remembering he

had to use her formal name. "I was desperate. I'll give it back to you tomorrow. I left it at my aunt's."

Jackie touched him lightly on the arm, it was like a butterfly landing on his skin. His throat tightened and his skin jangled at her touch. "Don't worry, Patty, I reported it as lost and I have a replacement. I forgive you. Elizabeth explained to us that you're very confused at the moment. We have to be gentle with you during your transition."

His stomach butterflies fluttered at seeing her huge innocent eyes. A glimpse of white teeth glistened from behind her open glossy lips. They seemed ready at any moment to bestow a gentle kiss on him. He imagined those lips around his penis and closed his eyes without thinking. A knot formed in his throat and a tingle flowed into his penis.

Jackie's eyes rested on his long pink nails. Then her words came back to him about him being confused. "What confusion, what transition?" he asked.

Jackie flicked her head back to stare at her desk computer screen. "It can't be easy. Your hormones must be all over the place. I guess that's why your feminine style today is somewhat..." she thought for a moment, digging deep in her mind for the right word. Then a glint of satisfaction in her eye as it came to her. The fluorescent light above her seemed to have lit up her brain cells. "Exaggerated."

He stared at her innocent face as Jackie concentrated on her screen. "And what transition did Elizabeth suggest I might be experiencing?"

Jackie stopped typing and swivelled on her chair to face him. "Your change to a woman of course. Your wife told us all about how you always knew you were a girl inside and how much this affected you. You're brave to come out as a girl. She told us how difficult it was for her too, having a feminised husband, but she had made a marriage commitment and she's going to stick by it. She said she wasn't going to hide from helping you. She's so kind. You are very lucky to have Elizabeth as your wife." She leaned over and planted a wet kiss on his cheek.

"What, I.... no..." His words wouldn't come out. He didn't want to be a girl, what was Elizabeth playing at now? "I am not a girl inside, I'm a man."

Jackie stroked his hair, running her fingers through the strands. "She told us there were days you challenged your belief you wanted to be a girl but this was natural. You have to overcome many years of living as a man and overcome social pressure. We will encourage you to embrace your femininity." She stared into his eyes and his stomach turned in delight. "I'm here for you, Patty, to help you become the girl you want to be."

He swallowed hard, his mouth was dry. He was speechless. Jackie was convinced he wanted to become a girl. Nothing he could say was going to change her mind. Elizabeth had got to her first. His enforced transition had no barriers.

Chapter 6 – Feminised and pretty naked

It had been an awful day in the office and he did not want his wife's nonsense now he was home. The office women had mocked him without a break. Jackie was convinced he wanted to become a real girl; she gave him tips on how to be more feminine. Then he'd have to travel home on the train. Dressed as a schoolgirl.

Patrick sat on the bed in his bedroom while Clara stood over him. She relayed Elizabeth's instructions. Clara was a mini-Elizabeth wannabe, even parroting her voice mannerisms. He had renamed Clara the robot in his mind.

He longed for the days as an itinerant musician. Freedom was something that no longer existed. He had no peace and no privacy.

Clara's voice melted into the background. He'd had an awful day listening to the women in the office mock him. They had told him how they liked his new schoolgirl style, how pretty he was, how they loved his hair colour and his new nails.

They told him how brave he was to venture out into the world looking like a girl.

The women meant well, he supposed. It helped that his penis was not exposed any more reminding everyone he was a male. In truth, his feminisation was not as terrible as he pretended it was. The evidence was his huge erection hidden beneath his skirt: it felt damn good.

Jackie had lent him her sunglasses for his journey home. They had helped him to hide away from the world and the stares on the tube train. He didn't know whether the stares were for his schoolgirl look or that he retained something male about him. It was probably both.

Elizabeth was due home soon and had phoned ahead to give Clara instructions for him. Clara repeated them. No clothing was to be permitted at home that night. She wanted him naked. He would have preferred to wear the skirt. He liked his skirt, although he wasn't about to let that nugget out.

Elizabeth expected him naked at home but now there was a change. His nudity had been when they were alone. Clara was there that evening. "Off with your clothes, Patty," she said.

"Strip off."

He thought about the lovely Jackie so he could tune out Clara's hectoring voice. Clara was a cold robot. He thought about shaking her, asking for her own opinion. She should have her own mind, not repeat what Elizabeth wanted. Did *she*, Clara, want him naked? He wasn't sure what went on in her mind apart from blindly following Elizabeth's instructions. It was little wonder Elizabeth liked her so much.

Elizabeth expected everyone to follow her instructions. Her way was the law. One law was that she wanted Patrick to be humiliated and feminised. He'd made one tiny indiscretion. A drunken indiscretion overheard by Elizabeth. What did she expect? She was filthy rich and old. Well, nearly fifty, that was old to him. What did she think he had seen in her apart from her money? It was true, he did want her money. She'd caught him and she'd had her fun. He'd taken her punishment on the chin it was time to stop. Enough was enough.

"Clothes off, Patty. Elizabeth will be home in five minutes and she wants you naked when she gets here." Clara moved closer, invading his face.

He leant back from her. "Isn't it time this finished, Mistress Clara? I've served my punishment."

"Finished?" Clara said, her eyes bulging.

She was not bright, he thought. A soldier following orders. Clara chewed over his question.

She came to a conclusion. "This isn't about punishment, Patty. Elizabeth chose you for this. It's not finished, it's just starting."

It was Patrick's turn to be dumbstruck. Heat rose through his body. The room was suddenly too warm. *Just starting?* At that moment the metallic sound of a key sliding into a lock sounded from downstairs.

Clara looked panicked. She slapped Patrick with spite across his cheek. "That's Elizabeth. Clothes off, now." Clara's voice cracked. She liked to ensure her boss was satisfied and Patrick was being stubborn. He didn't move. "Clothes off or I promise you a severe punishment. You'll be working naked in the office tomorrow. There will be no pretty skirt to cover you. You choose Patty."

Her comment hit him harder than her slap. Elizabeth was

ruthless and this would happen without her missing a beat. Clara glared, her black sensible trousers hung on narrow boyish hips. Her shoes were flat and wide. She ran a hand through her dark-brown thick hair. He watched the impatience fuse through her. He had no choice. He unbuttoned his blouse. A hint of satisfaction flashed on Clara's face.

Elizabeth called up from downstairs, "Where are you, Clara?"

Clara turned her head to the doorway behind her. "I'm overseeing Patty as she takes her clothes off, Elizabeth. I won't be a minute."

Her hard face glared back at Patrick. She ran a hand through her hair again and lowered her voice. "I'll cover up your insolence this one time but a warning. The next time you don't follow my orders, you won't believe the world of shit I'll put you in. Do you understand me?"

Patrick slipped off his blouse to reveal his smooth flat bare chest and lowered his head. "Yes, Mistress Clara." This was not the time to be clever. His rebellion would wait.

He stood and unzipped his skirt. It fell to the floor, in a heap around his ankle socks. Clara's eyebrows raised a tiny bit then fell. His penis hung loose. His erection had gone in the face of the hated Clara. She glared at his penis. He wanted to close his legs around it, to hide it from her glare.

"You can keep your pretty little white socks on. And put your shoes back on. Otherwise, you're to remain naked." She looked him up and down one more time. "I want you downstairs in a minute to serve Elizabeth a drink or whatever she asks for. I used to do this for her but these tasks will fall to you now. Elizabeth wants to relieve me of these mundane chores."

Clara left his room and went downstairs. He heard the muffled greetings as they spoke to each other at the foot of the stairs.

Elizabeth wants, Elizabeth wants, that's all he ever heard from the robotic Clara. He kicked his grey skirt away and it slid under his single bed. His soft penis bobbed with the movement. He fixed on his smooth legs, pretty socks and shoes. Horrible. Maybe.

"Patricia?" A shrill shout came from Clara. "Elizabeth wants some fresh coffee. Now."

Elizabeth wants, Elizabeth wants. He kicked out at the closest object. His bed frame.

"Patricia." Clara's voice was more urgent.

He trudged to the doorway and the smell of cooking flowed up from downstairs. He hadn't heard Elizabeth's cook arrive. She was a jolly middle-aged motherly woman called Margaret. She had often giggled at Elizabeth's manner with him. Margaret had a host of clichéd comments about their relationship.

She made her comments with a knowing smile and a touch of her nose: *I can see who wears the trousers in your relationship* or *you're certainly under her thumb.* The most annoying one every time Elizabeth told him off was, *"You can be right or you can be happy, Patty."* He was sure he was about to get another one of her pearls of clichéd wisdom.

His white socks with the frill and female shoes added a layer of ignominy to his abject humiliation. He thought about ripping them off but that would be in spite to himself. They provided some comfort for his cold feet. Elizabeth had never told him to be naked when another woman was around before. Now he had Clara and Margaret to deal with. Elizabeth was ramping up his humiliation. It wasn't as if Clara hadn't seen his penis and balls before. This time he felt more exposed, more submissive. Naked for the evening. Except for the shoes and socks.

He was lost in feeling sorry for himself and hadn't heard Clara coming back up the stairs. She appeared in the doorway, tapping a long wooden spoon against her trouser leg. Tap, tap, tap.

"I warned you, girl. She strode in and pushed his head down. She swiped the spoon twice across the top of his thigh. *Slap slap*. He bent in shock, his hands went to the reddening thigh. Slap, another swipe, this time across his bare bum cheeks. He bent back, throwing his hands against Clara's rain of wooden spoon slaps now hitting him.

He put his hands in the path of the arc of the spoon. Clara switched her attack and lifted her wooden spoon weapon in an upward arc. It caught the bottom of his balls square on.

Patrick danced around the room as Clara spanked again. His hands cupped his penis and balls. Clara paused, hands by her sides and the wooden spoon tapping against her black trousers. Patrick remained doubled up, his hands on his genitals, breathing heavy, eyes watering.

His eyes fell to the floor, he couldn't face her angry face. A sharp pain grabbed his ear. She was twisting it down. She pulled him out of the room holding his ear, keeping it twisted. He tugged his head back which only received a stronger twist on his ear. He felt a new jolt of pain; it was as if she was going to twist it off. His resistance faded. He allowed her to pull him down the stairs and into the kitchen, head down, back arched and his eyes to the floor.

There was a sudden relief as Clara released her grip. He pulled himself up. Elizabeth was sitting on a high stall at the breakfast bar, still in her work suit. She crossed her legs amplifying her defined leg muscles through thin glossy black stockings. She was in four-inch heels on patent-black court shoes.

Elizabeth flicked her head to throw back her mane of

tussled long brown hair. She wore black-framed glasses, a design name etched in silver script along one arm. Elizabeth needed glasses for reading but didn't like to wear them at any other time. He'd seen her squint to read rather than put on glasses when others were with her. The glasses gave her an air of authority. He liked it.

A clatter of metal pots caught Patrick's attention. His body slumped. Margaret the cook was preparing dinner. She was not phased by the sight of him naked, she was getting on with doing the dinner. A *none of my business* expression was plastered across her face.

Elizabeth's gaze washed over him and settled on his bare penis and balls. Patrick closed his eyes for a moment; he was nothing more than a plaything for her.

"I have a new rule for you, girly." Elizabeth's voice cut into the silence. "Whenever you enter a room, I want you to curtsey to any women there. You can start now and then prepare some fresh coffee for me and Clara and bring it into the living room."

Elizabeth waited, Clara's eyes flitted from her to Patrick.

Rules, rules he thought. He longed for his life before without rules. That was long gone.

"One leg behind the other and bend from the knee. Arms out as if holding an invisible dress. Head bowed. Now, girly."

Clara raised the long wooden spoon. He held his breath before exhaling. He bent at the knee as his wife had told him. His penis pushed out into a semi-erection. In his horror, it pointed to his wife as he curtsied to her. Her face gave no reaction. He raised himself in horror at what she had made him do. He sauntered to where the coffee was stored. Margaret ignored him.

"Ahem," coughed Elizabeth. He froze, fighting a growing erection. There was something intoxicating about his wife humiliating him with Clara watching and Margaret pretending not to. He did not want this erection but his penis was not obeying his mental orders. It was obeying Elizabeth's.

"I said you will curtsey to any woman when you enter a room. You curtsied to me but Clara and Margaret are still waiting."

"Don't worry about me, dear," Margaret said without

turning around. "Just make sure he keeps his *little fellow* away from any hot surfaces. And any drips from the food."

This can't be happening, he thought. Elizabeth wanted him to curtsey naked to Clara and then Margaret, the middle-aged frumpy cook? It was unthinkable. A lot of unthinkable things were happening to him. Clara raised the wooden spoon. He faced her and curtsied, his erection was now full and firm. Clara his nemesis had satisfaction bathed over her face. The plain girl had no thoughts of her own. Margaret's pretence at normality fell away. She glanced up from chopping vegetables. He curtsied to her too. She put a hand to her mouth, her eyes creased. "Oh my gosh," she blustered.

It couldn't get any worse than this, he thought. Things were going to get a whole lot worse.

Chapter 7 – Maid time

Patrick's back ached. He stood in the corner of the living room with his hands on his head. He'd been there for over half an hour. He faced out towards Elizabeth and Clara, his erection hard and firm.

Elizabeth was punishing him for complaining about curtseying. He hadn't said anything but Elizabeth had spotted his eyes rolling.

A gentle draught blew against his erect penis and around his smooth balls. It was as if a tiny moth's wings brushed against his exposed skin. He wanted to scratch but knew better. His tormentors' empty coffee cups were on a wooden coffee table between them. Elizabeth sank back in the armchair. Her eyes flowed over Patrick for a short moment with a look of distaste.

Clara was sitting upright as if she were waiting to be released from the headmistress's office.

Elizabeth spoke. "Time to get moving."

Patrick removed his hands from his head and slumped in relief. His back was sore.

"I have a guest coming for dinner." Said Elizabeth. A sneer washed over her face.

Patrick gasped. *No, she couldn't do this.* It was one humiliation after the next.

Elizabeth spotted his distress. "I' don't believe my guest will want to see your little clitty swishing around. I'll allow you to get dressed for this evening."

Relief coursed through him. Thank goodness, he thought. Clara bounced out of her chair and left the room. It was the signal she had been waiting for. Patrick didn't care if she put him in a dress or a mini-skirt as long as he wasn't naked. He was certain her guest would laugh at him in a skirt but it was becoming a question of degrees of humiliation. Skirt humiliation was a whole level down from naked humiliation.

Clara returned to the room, her sour face broke into a smirk. She held a silk-like garment over her arm. Layers of lighter pink petticoats rustled under what was a dress of some kind. She held a shopping bag in the other hand. She handed the dress to Patrick who took it and held it out as if it was contagious.

"Patty dear," Elizabeth spoke. "You need to pay your way in my house. Your low-level job at my company is not enough to support my lifestyle."

He waited, expecting the worse. He held the pink silk dress to his stomach. It gave him some cover although the feel of the smooth silk hardened his erection further.

Elizabeth walked to him and glared down using her four-inch height advantage in heels. "Your additional job is to be my housemaid. You're going to serve Margaret's meal to my guest and me. You will not forget to curtsey to each of us as you enter and leave the dining room. That's one curtsey to me and one to my guest."

Patrick wanted to run, to scream, to shout at her. Nothing would help him and there was nowhere to run to. He was going to have to be a maid for the night. Clara tipped her shopping bag onto the coffee table. There was a pack of white stockings, a white suspender belt, pink frilly panties, a bullet-like pink rubber device and a pink plastic cage in the shape of a cock. A heart-shaped padlock hung from the catch of the pink cage. Patrick's eyes bulged. He glanced at the knickers. A small element of relief surged. The dress wasn't long enough to cover his penis but the panties would cover him. Just about. Clara put a pair of bright pink sandals next to him. He gasped at the heels. They looked at least three inches high. How would he walk in those shoes?

"Patty, be a good girl and put on these pretty maid clothes. Clara will help you with the cock cage and the butt plug. I need you filled up and locked away before my guest arrives. We don't want all your smelly bits and nasty holes leaking any messy stuff, do we? I'm going to get ready for dinner. My guest will be here in twenty minutes."

His submerged anger rose to the surface. He stuttered a complaint. "Please no. I can't wear all this."

A thwack came down on his bare bum cheeks. He jumped as much in surprise as pain. Clara had spanked him with her bare hand. Elizabeth moved into his face. She was an inch away, her coffee breath made his eyes water. Her eyes were hard and brown. Her lips drew back. She was like a cat ready to attack.

"This is going to happen, Patty, and there are two options. I unleash Clara on you to spank you until you won't be able to sit down for a week. Or you put everything on now. Choose now but be quick as I need to get ready. I want to look my best tonight."

Clara rubbed her hands together in anticipation. There was no doubt she relished spanking him hard. She was like a guard dog straining on a leash.

He dropped his eyes. "I'll put the clothes on."

Elizabeth remained in his face. "I'll put the clothes on, what?" Her voice pitch raised as if she were asking a question. Something was missing in his reply.

He had nowhere to run or hide. He had to give in to everything his wife expected. "I'll put the clothes on, *Ms Remington.*" He shuddered at having to call his wife by a formal name while she called him by a girl's first name.

Elizabeth remained there. He cringed and folded his chin into his chest.

"And you'll stand there nice and still while Clara fits your cock cage and butt plug."

He was ready for the reply this time. "Yes, Ms Remington." He was trapped. To survive for now he would need to follow everything Elizabeth told him and, by extension, Clara.

Elizabeth left and stomped upstairs to her bedroom. Clara grabbed the pink dress from him and placed it on a chair. She took the cock cage and pulled the ring around the back of his smooth balls without care. He fought back a cry as she pinched his loose skin, pulling it together. She took his penis and stuffed it into the plastic cage as if she were stuffing an onion into a plucked chicken carcass.

She clipped the metal heart-shaped padlock shut and then tugged it twice to check it was locked. She removed the two keys from the lock and clipped them onto a silver chain around her neck. A satisfied smirk grew on her face.

"Bend over, Patty."

What now he thought. He had to be submissive. It was his only option until Elizabeth got bored. One day he would look back at this. It would be a small chapter of his life. A mistake he had already paid for a hundred times over.

He bent over not knowing what to expect. A sensation hit his bum hole. He flinched and went to stand up again. A hand pushed on his back. Then he felt a painful searing feeling as something entered his anus. Clara had pushed something deep inside him. This was an invasion of his body and his indignation grew. Elizabeth had taken ownership of his body a while ago and was now sharing that ownership with Clara.

For now, he had no rights. He forced his anger to fall away, it served no purpose.

Clara pulled him up by his hair and he put a finger to his bum. There was a soft silicone flange across his cheeks. The edge of his bum hole stung.

"I could have used gel to make it easier but it might have slipped out again. I thought dry would be better. The stinging will go away," Clara said from behind him.

"Yes, Mistress Clara," Patrick replied.

"Put your pretty maid's clothes on now, Elizabeth's guest will be here in a few minutes. It will be your job to go to the door to let your wife's guest in."

Patrick didn't like that idea. But, it was no worse than

everything else that Elizabeth had made him do. Another woman would get to see him in a short humiliating dress. One more humiliation to add to the several others. His immediate concern was the discomfort. Walking in high heels with a piece of silicone in his bum and a plastic cage locked around his penis was not easy.

Clara hugged him around his waist. An odd embrace. She clipped something together and stepped back. It had been no moment of affection. She had snapped on a white suspender belt, the straps hung loose down the front and back of his smooth legs.

He pulled the little dress over his head and Clara assisted him in straightening it over his body. It hugged his slender frame as if measured and made for him. Perhaps it had. Two long wide ties hung from either side of the elasticated waistband. Clara pulled and tied it in a large bow against his back.

The tip of his cock cage poked below the several layers of white petticoats. The pink satin dress flared out like the tutu of a ballet dancer. The pink panties lay on the coffee table, taunting him. At least they offered the promise of cover. They had a thin g-string but never mind. He would be covered.

Clara picked the knickers up and passed them to Patrick. His penis was hard and rammed up against the large open slit at the end of his cock cage. The end part of his penis was visible. In some ways, it was worse as they provided a frame to display his vulnerable area. He pulled the panties over his feet and drew them up to his crotch. The g-string hit against his butt plug.

He tugged the panties up around the cock cage. They fell on either side of his cock cage. He froze for a short moment. They were open at the front. Crotchless. His smooth balls hung free and open behind the pink cage. Another humiliating frame for his once private parts. Displayed again for whoever was coming to dinner. Was it his aunt Melissa? He didn't want to see her ever again.

He pulled on the fine white glossy stockings and clipped the suspender straps to the tops. They kept falling out. He couldn't get the attachment button to remain in the clip. His fingers shook. Anger and panic. Why did they make these things so awkward?

"Let me do it, Patricia. Our guest will be here any minute." Clara bent on one knee and clipped the stockings into the suspenders. Her head was an inch from his cock cage, her hair brushed against the tip and his balls. His penis tried to expand further and hit against the sides of its prison. His penis head squeezed into the slit at the end. Clara spotted it. "Oh Patty, I didn't know you cared."

He didn't but the doorbell chimed and his thoughts transferred to another problem. The guest had arrived.

"Quick, girly, shoes on and go to the door to welcome our guest."

He slipped into the pink sandals. He tottered for a second trying to find his balance in the thin stilt-like heels. The doorbell chimed again. His clothes were tight and fussy, he was trussed up like an over-dressed chicken.

Clara picked up the discarded packaging for the stockings. "You'd better answer the front door, Patricia. Elizabeth's guest is waiting."

Chapter 8 – Dinner party

He staggered out of the living room, struggling for balance in his high heels. He made it to the front door. The doorbell chimed again, the guest was impatient. Patrick's ankle gave way on the heels. It was like walking on stilts. At three inches, they were not as high as his wife's shoes. How did she manage?

His chest sank at the thought of the guest being Aunt Melissa. Perhaps she had come to gloat. She would have much to gloat about, he was dressed in the most shocking outfit to date. Pinks and whites and frills. His dress was too short to be called a dress, more a top with a ridiculous frill around the waist.

A shadow behind the glazed glass of the front door paced.

"Just a second," Patrick called out."

It was near impossible to walk fast in these heels. It was near impossible to walk at all. The pink plastic cock cage was visible and leading the way, his penis rammed hard and firm inside. His white stocking tops were exposed, the suspender straps fixed tight across his bare skinny thigh. He put a hand on the handle. Maybe Elizabeth's friend wouldn't notice he was a male? His hair, nails, dress and his heels were not what a man wore. He had no boobs but he was slim and not too tall. Maybe he'd pass as a girl.

The hall mirror's reflection taunted him. His platinum blond hair, styled in a thick long bob, flowed down his neck. His appearance was feminine. Too feminine. It was a caricature. His arched thinned eyebrows gave him an expression of permanent surprise.

He pushed on the door handle. He spotted his fingernails; a quarter of an inch long and covered in gloss-pink varnish. He studied his face in the mirror as he delayed the humiliating exposure to his wife's friend. She was to be the latest woman to laugh at him. It was becoming a parade.

Horror suddenly filled him. His face was unmade. He had no make-up on. He'd forgotten. Everything about him screamed feminine and girl. Except for his face.

His stomach knotted. Elizabeth's guest was going to see a male face on a female body. He let go of the front door handle.

The guest rapped on the glass seeing Patrick's silhouette behind at the door. It was no good he was going to have to let her in.

He told himself to remember to curtsey. Elizabeth's new rule; curtsey to all women. He had to remember to hold the edge of his dress as Elizabeth had instructed. His hand went back to the door handle again. He breathed in and then out. Calm down, he told himself, it's just one more woman. He twisted the door handle down and pulled the door back towards him.

He stepped back, head down. It was the best way to hide his masculine face. He hid behind the door, delaying his big reveal and to avoid any neighbours catching a flash of his pink satin. He looked to the floor. The guest walked in; a ripple of cool outside air and the clean smell of autumn leaves followed in the wake.

Patrick felt eyes bearing down on him. He kept his own eyes to the floor. He would let them get a feel of the rest of his humiliating outfit first. That was bad enough. It was time to curtsey. His hands went down to take the edges of the petticoated layers of his dress. He lost balance on his new higher heels and steadied himself. He curtsied and held his position low. If he stayed low maybe the guest would go into the living room.

The guest's presence loomed over him. Standing, unmoving. Then a deep-throated laugh. Patrick's head shot up. Elizabeth's guest was in a sharp light-grey suit. A powder blue shirt was unbuttoned and exposed a tanned muscular chest with dark hairs. Teeth sparkled in the hall light, black hair brushed back, a hint of a quiff with short grey flecks at the sides. It was a man. "Loved the curtsey."

Patrick's mouth went as dry as desert sand.

The man's blue eyes creased and twinkled. Their eyes locked. "Pleased to meet you, Patricia." The man's mouth twisted up in one corner, stifling a broader grin. He had a hand in one pocket, the other hung loosely by his side. A professional man, educated. Possibly an actor.

He knew Patrick's feminised name. This wasn't good. Elizabeth must have explained the situation to him. But who was he? Why was he here? The two faced each other for a few seconds more; Patrick was frozen in shock. Despite Patrick's three-inch heels, the man towered over him.

"Are we going to stay here looking at each other or are you going to show me through to your beautiful wife?" The man's eyes sparkled hinting at a stronger amusement inside.

"Er, come this way, sir." Patrick glanced behind as tottered to the living room. This stranger knew everything.

Patrick showed the man into the living room where Clara was waiting, standing. Patrick remembered to curtsey to her while averting his eyes from the man's face. He imagined more retrained amusement and did not want to see it. This was not the humiliation of the office which had a certain excitement mingled up with the horror. This was simply horrible. A man.

He held back at the door and the man strode past him, tall and confident. He shook hands with Clara and then they kissed each other on the cheeks. "Good to see you again, Dan. Elizabeth will be down in a moment."

They knew each other. Patrick decided that this showed Dan to be a business associate. That was it. Patrick rubbed at his temples, he had a headache. Elizabeth had excelled herself with her latest humiliation. It was one thing to show him up to her female employees but to denigrate him in front of another man was simply horrible.

"Patricia, would you ask Mr Hunter what he'd like to drink." Clara waited. "You're not being a very efficient housemaid are you?" Her eyes twinkled.

Dan Hunter raised one eyebrow. "I'll have a single malt. Something from one of the Scottish Islands. I'll let you choose which one. Thank you. Elizabeth said you were generally well-behaved."

Patrick's mind raced. Amongst this horror show, was Mr Dan Hunter being polite to him? And what was a single malt? Scottish? Was it a type of beer? That used malt didn't it? Or was that hops? He couldn't remember He only drank beer, what could he know about spirits? Elizabeth's kept her alcohol in the kitchen, she wasn't a big drinker. It got in the way of long hours working and in the way of innovative business thinking. She was such a bore. Patrick could do with a beer himself right now. He moved towards the kitchen. He would ask Margaret what a single malt was.

A curt call from the living room stopped him dead. Clara. "Patty, haven't you forgotten something?"

Oh no. She expected him to curtsey to her with Dan Hunter watching with his irritating amused smirk.

"Where's the curtsey?" she asked.

When would this humiliation nightmare end? He trudged back into the living room. Clara stood hard with her arms folded. He expected her to start tapping her foot at any moment. He had to get this over with. He curtsied and stood straight again. He was about to leave.

"Patty."

He stopped in his tracks. "Yes, Mistress Clara."

"And Mr Hunter..?"

He waited for her to finish. *And Mr Hunter what?* Sometimes Clara spoke in riddles she expected him to complete by telepathy.

"Mr Hunter is Elizabeth's guest tonight. You need to curtsey to him too. What on earth is wrong with you tonight?"

Dan Hunter stifled a giggle. Patrick's temple thumped. Curtsying to a man. The first time was an accident, he had expected a woman. This was not good. Uncool. But he had no choice either. He thought about Clara's revenge. The spanking he'd receive if he didn't do this would be worse and probably in front of Dan. Get it over with quickly and move on, he told himself. He dipped his curtsey conscious of his cock cage protruding straight at Dan Hunter.

More horror filled him as Dan Hunter gave a short polite clap. "Well done, Patty."

This was not good, thought Patrick. This was not good at all.

He tottered to the kitchen, his calves feeling the strain of his heels. His head thumped. The smell of Thai food from a deep bubbling frying pan reminded him he hadn't eaten. That would have to wait. Margaret's back was towards him as she concentrated on the cooking. He was not going to curtsey to the frumpy Margaret now he was out of sight of Clara.

He ticked off a minor victory as Margaret was too busy to notice or care. He asked her what single malt was. She told him it was a Scottish whisky and Elizabeth kept it in the kitchen cabinet by the back window. She spoke without glancing back at him, deep into her culinary activities.

Patrick found the spirit bottles in the cabinet and chose one with the most Scottish-sounding name. He poured a shot and thought about taking a huge swig. He resisted and, after adding some ice, tottered back to the living room. His calves were killing him and his toes were sore as his feet slid towards the front of the shoes. He mused on how women could ever wear high heels and be comfortable. He entered the living room to find Dan Hunter and Clara standing together talking. Elizabeth had yet to appear. They ignored him as he approached. He wobbled towards them in the unfamiliar heels.

He stood by them waiting for them to register his presence. Dan stopped speaking and glanced at him and shaped to take his drink. Clara barked, "Curtsey."

He dipped his curtsey to Dan Hunter and then faced Clara and repeated it. Blood flushed into his face, this was as bad as it got. Genuflecting to a man while dressed in a dress that didn't cover him with his exposed cock caged in pink plastic.

Dan Hunter took his drink. "Thank you, Patty," he said kindly.

What a polite man, he didn't have to be like that, thought Patrick. Patrick felt a mild endearment for this man who was not grinding him down further. That was some good news. Dan's eyes left Patrick towards a place behind his shoulder. A wide smile came over Dan's broad face. His teeth gleamed like a toothpaste commercial. Patrick wondered if this Dan had porcelain veneers, they were so perfect.

Dan shot past Patrick. Elizabeth had entered the living room silently. Patrick's heart missed a beat when he saw her. She was stunning. She wore a black cocktail dress with no shoulders. It was held up purely by her expansive breasts. The dress fanned out from her waist in voluminous pleats. It finished an inch below her knees. She wore four-inch black sandals and diamond earrings dangled from her earlobes.

Somehow she had done her hair within ten minutes. It flowed and waved and cascaded over her bare shoulders and tumbled down her back.

Dan and Elizabeth hugged affectionately. That was something more than business partners, Patrick noted. A handshake would have been sufficient. Dan and Elizabeth swapped glances, holding on to each other's forearms. They spent a moment looking into each other's faces and then they kissed on the lips. They held it for a couple of seconds. That was more than a business partner kiss. Or was it? Elizabeth tucked her arm in Dan's and led him through to the dining area.

As Elizabeth passed Patrick she said without taking her eyes off Dan, "Close your mouth, Patty."

He shut it tight, his teeth clattered together.

"This is a business meeting. Right?" he said to no one in particular.

"Ha," Clara snorted, overhearing his mumble. "Whatever gave you that idea, Patty?"

Chapter 9 – Feminised and cuckolded

Patrick hadn't expected to be jealous. He hadn't imagined Elizabeth was going to do anything more than have dinner at home with Dan Hunter. Patrick fumed as he sat at the breakfast bar, a hand on his chin. It wasn't easy to sit in the petticoated dress as it refused to lay flat. And it was too short to cover his cock cage.

What had Elizabeth been thinking when she made him wear this, he asked himself? Utter humiliation and in front of a man. He stewed in the kitchen as Margaret scuttled around him. She was not interested in his problems.

Elizabeth's dinner party with Dan had finished thirty minutes ago. Serving had been Patrick's task for that evening. He had served dinner and drinks in the stupid little dress while his wife flirted with the impossibly handsome Dan Hunter. Patrick expected Dan to leave shortly. It had been a demeaning evening. Yet that had been exciting. How could something so demeaning be so exciting? He shook his head as he considered this bewildering question.

Clara hadn't explained who Dan was. They were more than business associates, that was certain. Elizabeth had always been enigmatic but now she was worse. She threw back his questions with more questions. She was annoying him more and more with her approach. At the same time, this was not unpleasant. He enjoyed Elizabeth and Clara treating him as a child, it was a relief. No responsibility, he did what she told him to do. There was no need to tax his brain or think. He couldn't recall ever seeing her look so good, *even at her age.*

It was a relief to put his feet up on the stool. He had blisters on his toes which were rammed into these horrible high heels. His calves and thighs screamed pain at him. The odd thing was Dan *'tooth commercial'* Hunter had been the perfect gentleman with him. Dan had a sparkle of mischief in his eyes and a rictus actor-like smile. Dan was far too smooth and self-satisfied but he'd accepted Patrick's curtseys with a polite nod of acknowledgement.

Patrick wanted to hate him for the mumbled conversations

with his wife and for their hand touching across the table But he couldn't. Dan had behaved better than his wife. *Like a proper gentleman.* Elizabeth had giggled like a schoolgirl, her eyes sparkling. He had never seen her like that before. He thought she may have drunk too much. That was not like her. She had relaxed with this stranger. A stranger to Patrick but not to Elizabeth, that much was sure. She had never acted like that with him at any time in their relationship. Relationship? That wasn't the right word for what they had.

The worst of all was that he had found it hard to take her eyes off her tonight. He'd rediscovered a new yearning for her. One not based on her money and one that hadn't existed before. Everything that she had done to him that evening was exhilarating. Her pièce de résistance was making him serve her dinner guest in a short maid's dress. He hated the dress but he loved it too.

Sparks tingled across his skin. He hated serving them but he had been permanently hard inside his pink cage. Or he would have been if the tight cock cage had allowed him to burst free. His erection dug in like a restricted balloon.

Elizabeth had a spark in her eyes in the evening that had been missing during their short courtship and marriage. She was attractive for an older woman. She was too old for Patrick, or so he'd thought. Tonight, she was stunning. She had been dominant with him, treating him like a domestic servant; a domestic *feminised* servant. He hated himself for his feelings and thoughts. He shouldn't be enjoying her humiliation or having any feelings for her. But he loved her humiliating him. She had uncovered something he didn't know existed. Something she had seen in him.

Patrick's balls ached. He wanted to cum thinking about the evening. He was ashamed but his desperation for release covered that shame. Once Dan Hunter left, he would go to his small bedroom and masturbate. Assuming Clara released him from the cage. He would imagine Elizabeth telling him he was a stupid and useless girl. His penis pushed against its prison at the thought. He put his hand there. It was encased, imprisoned in pink plastic. He was desperate to touch it, to rub it. To open the dam and burst out.

Was it normal to masturbate while thinking about your

wife humiliating you? That wasn't normal especially as he had only wanted her for her money. The entire situation that evening had been odd, bizarre. But this release was for later. Now, he was still the maid for the two diners; his wife and her enigmatic handsome guest.

Elizabeth called from the living room; she wanted another single malt whisky for Dan Hunter and a cognac for her. They were now sitting together on the sofa in the living room. The lights were dimmed and music swayed lightly in the background. Margaret flashed past him in a bluster. She called out '*bye Patty*' and rushed through the front door. Clara had left a couple of hours ago. The kitchen clock ticked on inexorably towards midnight.

Patrick had a sudden thought. He would offer to call a taxi for his wife's guest. That was a great idea he thought. He stood up, his petticoats ruffling as he straitened them out. That would hurry Dan Hunter out of the door without appearing to be obvious. The evening had been unexpectedly exciting but he was tired and it was enough now. Plus he needed to get the cock cage off and masturbate. He touched his cage again, desperate to feel his skin. The hard plastic was no substitute. A warm sticky pre-cum dripped from the end onto his fingers exacerbating his intense desire for relief.

Patrick had removed his high heels to relieve the aches and pains screaming through his legs and feet. He put the shoes back on, it was what Elizabeth expected. His toes hurt. It was like he was balancing on the balls of his feet with his toes in a vice.

He made Elizabeth's and Dan's drinks and strode as best as possible to the living room. The only sound apart from the clip-clop of his heels was light jazz from the speakers. The door was partially closed and he pushed and entered without waiting.

Elizabeth sat up with a jerk. Dan was sitting bolt upright already. A fit of deep jealousy shot through him. She had been laying with her head on his lap. It was intimate. His wife brushed down her ruffled hair and then tugged down at the hem of her dress. She sat too upright, too fake. Patrick's eyes blinked and flashed over her, uncomprehending. Elizabeth's hair was messy, like a bird had nested in the back of it. He had never seen her with a hair out of place before, even after sleeping.

"Why didn't you knock stupid girl? Who do you think you are?" she snapped, her face flushed and reddened, her eyes narrowed.

Patrick was surprised by her irritation. She was covering up something and had lost some self-control. He sensed she had been doing something. Surely the inelegant sound of him stomping in his heels from the kitchen had been enough to warn of his arrival.

He told himself to stick to the original plan. He should show he accepted his new lower status and let her irritation flow over his head. She was probably tired and a little drunk. Perhaps she had been sleeping on Dan Hunter's lap, resting her head. Yes, that was it. Yet even that idea made his stomach ache. His constrained penis jerked, it liked her being close to another man. He hated that idea.

She was with a man far more masculine than him — taller and better looking. A successful man. The type of man he could never be; a fact amplified many times over by his ridiculous but wonderful petticoated maid's dress. It was time for it to stop now, though, all good things have their time limit. It was time to ease Mr Dan *smarmy* Hunter out of the door.

"I'm sorry, Ms Remington, I wanted to know if Mr Hunter would like me to call a taxi. It's nearly midnight." Patrick's hands strayed to the front of his dress and he linked his fingers together, feeling exposed. The exciting game was wearing thin. He was tired. He needed to put his aching feet and painful legs up in bed. After he had masturbated. That would help him sleep.

Elizabeth sat forward. "Stupid girl. Dan's staying the night. Leave the drinks on the coffee table and go away."

*Mr Smarmy was staying the nigh*t. He hadn't expected that. He told himself to stay calm. "Sorry, Ms Remington. I didn't realise. Would you like me to make up the spare room?" That would be what she expected, he was certain.

Elizabeth pushed her hands onto her knees and stood. Her hair stuck up in several places. "No. I don't want you to make up the spare room now go away you idiotic girl until I call you. Wait in the kitchen until I've finished what I was doing."

Finished? Finished doing what? What was his wife talking about? Elizabeth stared, waiting for him to go. She moved away from Dan, a broad grin was etched across his face. It widened further as Patrick caught his eye. Patrick's gaze fell and his mouth dropped open. Dan had a huge erection pointing to the ceiling from between unzipped flies.

Patrick stared at the erection in disbelief. Dan's hand moved onto it. He wrapped his fingers around it one by one. Dan's smile remained fixed and he winked at Patrick. Dan's perfect white teeth glinted from a single lamplight by his chair. Patrick backed away. He stumbled on his thin high heels. He flailed for something to hold onto. There was nothing; he fell backwards. Elizabeth sighed and turned away in exasperation. "OK. Watch if you must."

Patrick pushed himself up on his elbows, his legs apart, cock cage pointing up. Elizabeth took Dan's hand and guided him to his feet. Patrick's eyes widened seeing Dan's enormous erection, eight or nine inches. It was like a pirate's sabre. Elizabeth manoeuvred Dan sideways into Patrick's eye line. His wife knelt in front of Dan. The exposed end of the erect penis was an inch from her pursed expectant lips.

She breathed in deeply, closing her eyes, taking in Dan's sexual aroma. She wasn't going to suck him? Surely not, Patrick thought. That was a step too far. Her lips parted and hovered over Dan's long thick erect penis. Her eyes remained on Patrick. Dan's hand went to the back of Elizabeth's head and he pushed her onto his long rigid rod. Dan's head fell back as her lips formed a seal around it. Dan stifled a squeal. A knot tightened in Patrick's stomach.

Elizabeth's head moved back and forth along the length of Dan's erection, smears of lipstick coloured his cock light red. Dan moaned, louder this time. Patrick tried to tear his eyes away from his wife as she sucked another man's erection. It was an erection several times more impressive than his. He was glued to the horror he was watching, held by a terrible fascination.

His tiny penis was wedged against the plastic prison clamped around it. He grabbed the cock cage and tore at it but it was fixed firmly around his balls. It had been a reflex, he needed to cum. The end was jammed against the slit at the end, digging into his sensitive head. Pleasure and torture, torment and agony. It was trapped denying him any release and ejaculation. His enforced denial was desperate. He was trapped by the cuckold scene before him and his excited penis was imprisoned in the cage.

Dan shouted a long throaty, *yes,* as his body jerked several times. Elizabeth made sucking sounds like water exiting a bath plug. She sucked for several seconds as Dan's body relaxed. She withdrew her mouth and faced a startled Patrick, his mouth open in shock. She smiled and her mouth dropped open.

Patrick watched with horror as a dribble of Dan's viscous discharge dripped from one corner of her mouth. He followed its slow path to her chin. She caught it with the back of a finger then licked it away and swallowed. She licked her finger again slowly, nodded and mumbled a long humming sound. It was as if she had tasted a fine wine.

Chapter 10 – Go to your room

Patrick waited outside his wife's bedroom. The door was shut. It was the bedroom he had thought he would be sharing with his wife after their marriage. It was the bedroom his wife had banished him from.

Elizabeth and Dan Hunter went upstairs after she'd given him the blow job in the living room. Elizabeth had never given Patrick a blow job, even on their honeymoon. She had allowed Patrick to hump her and she had given him hand jobs but with a look of disdain etched on her face every time. He thought she didn't like giving blow jobs. She had liked giving one to Dan.

He knocked; whispers leaked from behind the closed door. He held a silver tray with two glasses of water on it, as Elizabeth had ordered.

"Come." It was Dan's deep baritone that invited Patrick into his wife's bedroom. The bedroom that should have been his. Patrick pushed on the door handle and stepped in.

Elizabeth and Dan lay on top of the bed, both naked and

sunken into the thick white duvet. Patrick's eyes were drawn to Dan's penis. It had recovered from his wife's blow job from twenty minutes earlier and was back to a nine-inch erect glory. Patrick was unable to avoid staring as Elizabeth wrapped her fingers around it. Dan shot his thousand-watt smile at Patrick. Dan opened his legs wider and his large balls hung loose on the white covers.

"You like my cock, girlie? Would *you* like to suck on it?" Dan gripped it with pride as Elizabeth ran her fingers over them and the erection. She moved in closer to it.

Patrick dropped his eyes to the floor. His face burned deep purple-red. Did he like Dan's cock? The image of Dan's erection burned in his mind. Disgusting, he thought. Elizabeth didn't seem to think so.

"It's not surprising your wife wants someone more manly, don't you think girly?" The polite Dan had melted away and to be replaced by a gloating Dan.

Patrick tried to ignore him and the fact that his wife had her full attention on Dan's huge erection. She planted a soft kiss on the end of it. Her tongue lashed out and wiped away a drop of pre-cum from the tip.

Dan wasn't finished with him. "Maybe you'd like to join us, girly?"

Patrick flinched. He wished Dan would stop calling him girly.

"You're more of a girl than a man," Dan said. "Perhaps you should bend over so I can take you up your tight little behind?"

Patrick glared at Elizabeth, willing her to tell Dan to stop. She was oblivious, not even listening. She was absorbed in Dan's cock.

"Your wife is a very sensual woman who needs a real man, not a girly husband." Dan pushed himself up onto one elbow as Elizabeth famed over his erection.

Patrick turned to leave the room. He could stand this no more. His excitement in the living room was replaced by the deep visceral horror at what he was witnessing. Dan had transformed into an arrogant monster, taunting him. His wife was acting as if Patrick wasn't even there.

"I.., I'll leave now." Patrick bowed his head and stared at the floor. He had to get out. This was demeaning and degrading.

"Stay, girly. I want you to see how a real man takes your sexy wife."

Why was she not taking charge? She had become passive while this brute of a man told him what to do and showed off. Patrick froze to the spot.

Dan manoeuvred Elizabeth so she was on all fours on the top of the bed. Dan moved behind her, his erection horizontal and strong, almost touching her waiting vagina. Patrick did not understand how his erection could be so firm when Dan had cum into his wife's mouth only a short while ago? Dan moved in and his cock slid into her glistening damp vagina. She let out a soft, "*Oh.*"

Patrick backed away. He wanted to tear Dan off his wife. This man had put his cock into his wife. Things had gone too far. A blow job was one thing but this was different. Patrick swayed on his heels as if he were drunk. Dan began to pump in and out. Slowly at first then faster. Elizabeth moaned and called out, "Harder, Danny, harder."

Patrick closed his eyes to the terrible scene unfolding

before him. His wife was being taken from behind by this arrogant man.

"This is how to service a real woman like your wife. She needs a proper cock inside her. A man's cock."

Dan pumped into Elizabeth with vigour. On and on it went, their moans grew and swirled around the room. Elizabeth called out for more. Then they stopped, frozen for a brief moment. They climaxed together, their backs arching like two fighting cats. Then they resumed their movement with less intensity as Dan drained himself inside Patrick's wife.

Dan pulled out and fell back onto the bed, his flaccid penis still a good eight inches and laying across one thigh. Elizabeth turned onto her back and lay beside him.

"You can go now, girly. Goodnight and I hoped you enjoyed seeing how a real man fucks me." Elizabeth's eyes were half shut, her voice dreamy and deep.

Dan waved Patrick away with a dismissive flick of his hand. Patrick backed against the door, he lost balance then recovered. His heart was pumping out of his chest and heat flowed into his neck and face. Was that despair or excitement?

He didn't understand his own emotions.

Elizabeth sat up on her elbows. "Patty?"

He stopped half in, half out of the doorway. "Yes, Ms Remington?"

"Don't forget to curtsey to us before you leave. Then wish us goodnight like a good housemaid."

Patrick wanted to scream. How dare they make him watch them make love and then insist he curtsey to them. But what could he do? Nothing. He curtsied to his wife. "Goodnight, Ms Remington." Then he turned to Dan and curtsied speaking through gritted teeth. "Goodnight. Mr Hunter."

Patrick stumbled out of the door and into the corridor. He placed his head and hands against the wall, breathing fast.

"Patty," said Elizabeth. "Come back here."

He straightened up and breathed out through pursed lips. He walked back in.

"You didn't thank Mr Hunter for satisfying me in a way you never could me. Thank him then curtsey again to him."

She had to be joking. They had subjected him to the most degrading night of his life and now she wanted to pile even more ignominy on him.

"I'm waiting, girly. You wouldn't want Mr Hunter to spank you. He's a lot stronger than Clara."

It was no joke and he had little option. He returned to the bedroom, the smell of damp sex pervading the air. "Thank you for satisfying my wife, Mr Hunter." He curtsied. The words caught in his throat.

Elizabeth and Dan Hunter exploded into laughter. Dan Hunter spoke. "Ask your wife if she enjoyed me fucking her, Patty."

Patrick wanted to scream out, *stop this*. His fists balled and he dug his nails into his palms until they hurt. He told himself to calm down. It would do no good to become so agitated. "Ms Remington." The next words choked in his throat. He spat them out. "Did you enjoy Mr Hunter fucking you?"

"Yes," she answered. Her eyebrows were raised while her eyes danced. "It was wonderful. Much better than anything you ever managed with your pathetic little worm."

Patrick fled the room. Laughter followed him as he

stomped away. Patrick entered his bedroom and slammed the door behind him. More muffled laughter followed. He tore off his high-heeled sandals and threw himself on his single bed. He was still in his tight maid's dress and white stockings. His throat constricted as he thought about what he had just witnessed and what he had had to say to them.

The dress was like a straitjacket, trapping him. Heavy sleepiness fell on him. His eyes drooped. Tomorrow was Saturday. He wouldn't have to go to the office dressed like a bimbo. He didn't think he would be able to sleep for a few moments despite the drowsiness. His eyelids shut and he fell into a deep troubled sleep.

Chapter 11 – Morning glory reflections

Patrick woke with a start. The low sun streamed through a gap in the curtains; a bright vertical line of light danced up the door. He sat up, disorientated. He'd dreamt he was back in his old apartment after a gig, smoking a joint. For a sleepy moment, he felt free.

He was no longer in that old life. He was in a virtual prison, trapped in a marriage with his wife in total control.

He rubbed his eyes. The pink bedroom walls taunted him, reminding him of what he had become. He was still dressed in his maid's dress; the stockings had twisted around his legs during the night.

The images of last night's humiliation played in his mind like a video recording on a loop. His wife's lips were around that man's cock. Her head moved back and forth along its length as her eyes glinted. He shuddered. The video movie in his mind moved on to Dan putting his enormous cock into Elizabeth from behind. Shame, ignominy and humiliation.

The red digits on the electronic clock clicked onto 11.12 am. He swung around and sat up on the edge of the bed. That was odd. Elizabeth never usually allowed him to lay in late. She usually had some task for him or something she wanted to do to him. Something humiliating that amused her. He needed to pee. First, he had to get out of these restrictive clothes. He pulled off the dress and unclipped the suspender, rolled off the stockings. He left them in a pile at his feet. He stamped on them. That felt better.

He padded out in bare feet to the bathroom next door, naked but for the pink cock cage locked around his penis and balls. His calves moaned after the evening spent in heels. Voices floated up from below. Female but too faint to make out. Elizabeth and Clara he guessed. He didn't care. He was beyond caring, he was taking the metaphorical punches as they came at him.

He raised the toilet lid and sat down. He breathed out in satisfaction as he peed. He had never thought about his future before. He had gone through life and let it fall where it took him.

When he played the guitar in bars, he used to dream someone would discover him. He hadn't ever pushed himself on any record companies or posted his music. That was too much bother; something would come up. Besides, his artistic ability was more important than success, wasn't it? It was true he played covers. No one wanted to hear his compositions. The bar and pub managers always told him to play popular tunes. He hadn't had a plan. He took the opportunities as they turned up. The opportunity had arrived but it had not been what he had expected.

He used to think Elizabeth coming into that bar and giving him her contact details was his big break. A rich woman was prepared to marry him. What could go wrong? Looking back Elizabeth had always been odd. She had wanted him naked at home from the beginning. She liked his hair long and his nails manicured. The signs had been there.

He finished peeing and kicked the toilet base in frustration. Pain shot along his big toe. He was too passive he told himself. It was time to grow up and take responsibility for his future. If not he would end up as his wife's own personal live Barbie doll to dress up and play with. He had drifted in life and drifted into this situation. It was his fault.

He stomped back to his room and closed the door. He repositioned his cock cage which was chaffing around his balls. He was hungry and thirsty. Breakfast would be nice. He sat back on the bed, his desire to be away from his wife greater than his desire for sustenance at that moment. He didn't know what to do about his marriage. He was trapped there with Elizabeth. She held every card. He relied on her for money, food and shelter. Without her, he would be homeless, jobless and on the street.

The question he faced was, should he remain there and put up with her humiliations or escape and take his chances? The other question he asked himself was whether he enjoyed the humiliations. He had enjoyed some of them last night and now he was angry with himself for it. What kind of man was he? Elizabeth had probably answered that question for him.

He thought about his guitar. Elizabeth had arranged the removal of his belongings from his old apartment. She had told him his things were all in storage. If he had a guitar he could find work. But that was out of the question as she had it stored away somewhere. The same with his clothing. If he left the house he would have to dress as a girl, as he had been when he had escaped to his aunt's house. All he had was very feminine clothing.

On the other hand, if he accepted Elizabeth's rules he might be comfortable. He had a house to live in, food and clothing. And female clothing. That had its attractions. He had to admit that it was not so bad to wear female clothes. Who would have thought that it would be much nicer than men's clothing? That had been a surprise. Or maybe a transgender? Was he a closet transvestite? Maybe not so much in the closet now.

What would be so bad as letting Elizabeth do what she wanted with him? Yesterday had been difficult but it had had an attraction too. Somewhere in his brain, he retained an old-fashioned notion that Elizabeth was his wife and she should not be having sex with other men. The reality was that she was his wife in legal terms only, not in the way they lived their lives. He was no more than her servant and plaything. Would it be so bad if he gave in and allowed her to do as she pleased? She would do it anyway so why not make it easier for himself? The easy path was attractive for him.

The path of least resistance was the one he always chose in life. That was the path he had taken since coming back from his abortive escape to his aunt's. That was his plan, to have no plan as usual. He would let Elizabeth decide for him and to do as she pleased. He would leave his fate to his wife. It couldn't get any worse than what she had done so far. He had survived that.

He wondered what was going on. Why had Elizabeth allowed him to remain in bed? What was she up to now?

Chapter 12 - The Mistress plan

The grumbles from his stomach convinced him that he had to go downstairs to the kitchen to have breakfast. He searched his wardrobe: a line of skirts and dresses. He sighed and told himself to cheer up. Accept this feminisation, enjoy it and choose a pretty skirt.

He looked for a few moments and unhooked a mini with a gathered waist. It was white with large red rose prints over it. He slipped it on. He chose a plain white fitted cotton top. He checked himself in the mirror twisting side to side. He brushed his long blonde hair. It was pretty even if his face wasn't.

He stepped out of his bedroom and downstairs in his bare feet with a small spring in his step. Acceptance. The skirt was soft and brushed against his thighs making his skin tingle and his head light. He entered the kitchen and ran his hand through his long thick hair. Clara stood by the back window.

"Hello, Patty. How are you today?" she chirped.

Patrick stopped. This was confusing. It was only the other

day she was spanking him with relish and now she was being polite. He would never understand women. "I'm fine Mistress Clara, how are you?"

"Good thank you. When you've had breakfast come and see Elizabeth and me in the living room."

She brushed past him. Clara was in jeans and flat shoes. Patrick had never seen her in a skirt or a dress.

Clara stopped in the doorway. "Oh and Patty." She waited. The old harder face returned. "You know full well that Elizabeth doesn't like you to wear clothing unless she has guests. Have your breakfast but remove your clothes before coming through to see Elizabeth. Don't be long or I'll be coming to get you and you won't want that."

Clara whipped off again. Nothing had changed. He rushed down some cereal and a cup of tea. He removed his skirt and top as Clara had ordered. He stood, his pink cock cage his only cover. He steeled himself for meeting Elizabeth following last night's activities. He wondered how she would react He had seen a very different Elizabeth. She had never acted like that with him. He hoped Dan Hunter had left, he couldn't bear to see him again.

The door to the living room was closed. He thought about what he'd witnessed there last night and shivered. Patrick tapped lightly and waited. Female voices chatted behind the door. Elizabeth and Clara. And someone else. His stomach turned over twice. More humiliation. He steeled himself.

"Come in Patty." Elizabeth's deep voice rang out. He pushed through the door and curtsied, holding out the invisible dress with his eyes on the floor.

"Good girl, now come over here next to me." Elizabeth was acting as if last night never happened.

Elizabeth sat in a large armchair. Clara sat on the coffee table, legs apart. A woman was sitting in another armchair. Her legs were crossed and she was dressed in black. Her dress hugged a tall yet slim frame. Her bespectacled face had a coldness. Her long hair hung straight and brown below narrow shoulders. She seemed four or five years younger than Elizabeth; he guessed she was in her early forties.

The odd things was she was not surprised at seeing a young man enter the room dressed only in a pink cock cage. It was clear to Patrick that whatever it was that Elizabeth had planned next, it would not be good for him and that this woman was part of her plan.

Clara rose and unclipped his cock cage. His shrivelled penis and balls fell into the fresh air.

"So Fiona," said Elizabeth, "this is the raw material. I thought it best if you see what you have to work with rather than see her covered in a skirt."

Fiona stood. She glided over to Patrick. A sudden self-consciousness enveloped him. Naked with a strange woman who began to circle him as if sizing up her prey. She ran a fingertip over one of his nipples. She prodded his chest around it with a fingertip. She placed herself face to face and ran a finger down his face and over his chin. She prodded his lips and took a step back as her eyes ran down his body. They settled on his little penis. She placed a finger under it and lifted it. A tingle of electricity shot through him. He hadn't cum for some time.

"What would you like me to do with this?" the lady said.

Patrick tensed. That was an odd question.

Elizabeth appeared to give the question some consideration. "I'm not sure, Fiona. I don't have any use for it but at the same time, it amuses me to cage it and deny her. What do you usually do with their little winkies?"

Patrick bit his lip, telling himself not to say anything. Give in. Be pliant.

Fiona let his penis drop from her touch, pulling her finger away with distaste. "I have three approaches depending on what the owners prefer. Most owners like the thought of keeping it and using it for control purposes, as you mentioned. Chastity and so on. It's also good for games, you can do all sorts of fun things with it. The second option is the medication I give to remodel males that makes it shrivel and become useless."

Patrick stepped away. A moment of panic.

"Where are you going, girl?" Clara said as Fiona glared down at him imperiously. She wasn't used to misbehaviour of any kind.

Fiona cleared her throat. "Thirdly, cut it off and have it reformed into a vagina."

That was too much. "You are not going to cut my cock off or make it shrivel. Elizabeth, what is going on?"

Elizabeth nodded to Clara. She strode over at slapped Patrick hard across his face. He winced as she stooped to swipe at his bare cheeks. She then slapped his penis and balls hard. He doubled up. Clara returned to her perch on the coffee table as if nothing had happened.

"Do continue Fiona," said Elizabeth. "This is interesting."

Fiona returned to her chair and sat. "Yes, she is excellent raw material and ripe for improvement. Her behaviour and manner are not good, as evidenced by that little tantrum. But, physically, I can make her look like a real girl."

Patrick's eyes swivelled from Fiona to his wife. A wave of discomfort at being naked and exposed in front of the three ladies. Fiona was assessing him as if he was one of a herd of cattle at a market.

"Patricia," said Elizabeth attracting his attention, "Fiona Allerton is someone your aunt recommended to me. She specialises in the physical and mental improvement of males. You, Patricia, need a lot of improvement. Ms Allerton will be here regularly to help me to improve you. She has a great deal of experience in turning useless pathetic males like you into good girls. And that's what we want for you, isn't it Patty? For you to become a polite, submissive and pretty girl."

Patrick was stunned. His submissive behaviour was not having the effect he had anticipated. Far from becoming bored with her feminisation and humiliation of him, she was ploughing ahead with further changes. She was saying she wanted to turn him into a girl. His mind raced at all the implications, the questions he wanted to ask but would never be answered.

At that moment, he thought again about his past life as a musician; touring the pubs and bars playing for a few pounds a night. He had been free with no commitments and no responsibilities. The trouble had been he'd had no future and no money. Now he had no commitments and responsibilities but he had a comfortable life of sorts. And he had a future path for the first time. The trouble was, the future was becoming more and more feminine.

Chapter 13 - Mistress is pleased

"Patricia." Elizabeth glared at him. "Stop daydreaming and bring us all coffee while I discuss your future with Fiona."

Patrick curtsied and scurried away and into the kitchen. He prepared fresh coffee, conscious of his nudity. A shard of sunlight streamed in through the kitchen window and shone onto his smooth penis. Despite the clear skies outside it was cold and the heating timer had long since switched off. He shivered. His penis has shrivelled in the chilly air, his balls a single round dome. It looked more pathetic than usual due to the lack of pubic hair. The image of Dan Hunter's enormous monster of a cock flashed in his mind as a reminder and a comparison.

His bare feet slapped on the kitchen floor as he walked back with the coffee. He stomped back to the living room with a tray and three steaming coffee mugs. Three near-identical expressions of bland amusement greeted him as he curtsied. He was aware that the act of dipping in the curtsey pushed his little penis out. Fiona Allerton followed him assessing his movement and manner.

Patrick offered the tray of mugs to her first and dipped his head. She inspected his shrivelled cold penis. She looked from one side to the other, appraising it. She poked a fingernail under it and lifted then let it drop.

"It's quite pathetic Elizabeth. I recommend doing something about it. It's not as if she has any use for it."

Patrick backed away. He didn't like the way she was thinking.

Elizabeth gave out a small snigger. "I haven't decided yet, Fiona, let me think about it."

There was a pause in conversation as Patrick served his wife and Clara. He retreated to one side and stood in silence.

Elizabeth sat forward, closer to Fiona, deep thought was written across her face. The expectant pause in conversation hung in the cool air. Patrick's hands strayed down to cover his penis. He moved his arms gently to avoid attracting Elizabeth's attention. He stood outside their circle, there but not there. He had nothing in common with these ladies, he was almost invisible as they chatted.

"So Fiona. Now you've seen Patricia and had a chance to see how she is, what is your proposal?"

Patrick tensed and shivered again. He was unsure if it was his lack of clothing or the implication of what Elizabeth was asking. He watched as this tall assertive lady with her skill in *male improvement* listened to his wife. He understood that changes to his approach to life were necessary. What was less comfortable were the changes that Elizabeth was making.

Fiona rose from her seat. She stretched up, erect, as if she had an invisible cane holding her head and back straight. She paced around the room. Patrick imagined her in front of a class giving algebra lessons. Long diamond and silver earrings dangled from her small neat ears. Her dark-framed rectangular glasses were slightly oversized.

"There are several things we need to do Elizabeth." She said. " I know it's great fun to humiliate them by exposing their little clitorises. However, in general, males need to wear pretty skirts and dresses and a bra at all times. I suggest we put her in these clothes now. If you like the idea of keeping her clitty on display or vulnerable, you can always put her in tiny skirts and no panties."

Anger balled up and constricted Patrick's throat and he wants to shout at Fiona. She's talking about him as if he were a pet dog or a young child. He yearned to run, to find his guitar and then lock himself away. He drew breath aware that Fiona was only getting started on her ideas of what to do to him. He was twenty-eight and had no family, few friends and nowhere to go.

His disappearance from the pub music scene had gone unnoticed. No one cared. He belonged to Elizabeth now. His body slumped, he had to take what Elizabeth wanted for him. Fiona was still pacing the living room, warming to her position as the subject matter expert. He guessed that this was a lucrative contract for Fiona Allerton.

Fiona stopped walking around and faced Elizabeth. "The second point is that high-heel training is vital. I strongly advise that you make her wear them every waking hour." Fiona waited for her point to sink in.

Elizabeth nodded.

"There are two reasons for this," continued Fiona. "One is that pretty feminine girls look much better in heels. Their legs become more defined and feminine. The second point is about bodily change. As we are transforming Patricia from a male to a female, several physical changes need to take place. The shortening of her calf and thigh muscles is one of the first physical changes we will work on. We need to put her in heels now. As soon as possible, you should purchase a couple of pairs of six-inch heels and keep her in them. You should probably buy a lock to ensure she keeps them on."

Patrick listened with anguish. This was going a lot further than he had expected. Fiona was talking about turning him into a real girl. He hadn't agreed to this. It was one thing to wear female clothing or to be naked. It was something else to transform his body. He had to say something.

"Excuse me, Ms Remington." Silence greeted his words." He swallowed and continued. "I don't want to be a female. I'll dress up for you in female clothing and I'll even be naked. I'll accept that you want other men. In return, I'll be quiet and respectful and even work at your offices. I don't like the idea of physical changes though."

Elizabeth scowled. "Shut up Patricia, you have no say in this. Not since you tried to double-cross me."

Patrick stared at the floor. He wished he could turn back time. Take back those words Elizabeth had heard him tell his friend. That he wanted to divorce her and take her for millions. He'd be happy to have his old guitar and apartment back. He'd even choose to be poor again.

Elizabeth's face remained angry as she turned to Clara and snapped. "Can you get something pretty for Patty to put on? And find those high heels too. Choose a tiny skirt. I want to keep her clitty vulnerable, it helps with control until I decide what to do with it."

Clara left and went upstairs. Patrick never expected that he would be looking forward to putting on a skirt and a female top.

"So onto my third point. Make-up. I see that Patty has no makeup. Nice nails and hair but no make-up." Fiona paused for effect.

"I thought that might make her too pretty plus I liked that

she had a vaguely male face," Elizabeth said.

"No no, my dear," Fiona said. "We need to use every female option we have to re-wire Patty's little brain towards femininity."

"OK, I can do that then. What more?"

"We need to re-sculpt her body. She's skinny but straight down. No curves." Fiona approached Patrick whose eyes widened in terror. Fiona put a hand around his nipple area. "She needs boobs. Large is best — 40, 42, maybe 44C or D cup. It's important to exaggerate them. It works better and the feminised girlies want it. They just don't know it."

Patrick stepped back. This was going too far. Fiona spun him around and put a hand on his bottom cheek.

"This bottom is far too flat. She needs these cheeks to be filled and rounded out." Fiona pulled Patrick around again and took his penis between two of her fingers. "We've spoken about this. You have to do something with this, Elizabeth. Male genitals are the root of all male evil. They guide their every thought and give them a false sense of masculinity. It's no cliché to say they think through their pathetic little thingies.

They are simple creatures and you are taking the right decision. I like to call it re-wiring. We will rearrange her into true femininity. At the very least she needs a cock cage. If not, she'll be playing with it and we don't want that do we?"

Elizabeth leant an elbow on her knee and rested her chin in her cupped hand as Fiona continued. "The male clitty does give us a method of control. Don't ever allow her to enjoy cumming. This leads to more submissive behaviour as her desperation grows. I can show you how to milk her without orgasm. If you do decide to go down the hormone route, it will be less of a problem anyway. It shrivels more and becomes useless. Another alternative is that when it's not caged, you can to dress it with pink ribbons and so on. Feminise it. You have to decide if you want to retain her clitty for control purposes or to get rid of it. The choice is yours."

Patrick's tongue stuck to the roof of his mouth as his mouth dried like out a desert in the midday sun. Elizabeth nodded. He couldn't believe she was taking this seriously. Would she consider cutting his penis and balls off? That was too far. It must be a threat to keep him on his toes.

"I'll keep her little clitty, Fiona. It's funny but I like the idea of a female girly with a tiny vestige of her past on display." Patrick breathed out noisily which caught Elizabeth's attention. She smiled. "I may change my mind though." He cringed.

Clara returned with a pile of clothing with a pair of shoes on top. She placed them on the coffee table. Fiona paced around the chair she had been sitting in. "I've outlined my plans. There's a lot more detail beneath this top-level approach. I can provide that detail if you agree to start on Patty's full feminisation programme. Here's a document describing each stage and my costs." Fiona passed a booklet to Elizabeth.

Clara sat on the arm of Elizabeth's chair as Elizabeth opened the booklet. Without taking her eyes away from the material she spoke out. "Patty get dressed while we look at this."

Patrick grabbed the pile of clothes with relish. He took the small white skirt and pulled it up. It was six inches long and he positioned it on his hips to cover his penis. He put on the white bra and a pink top. He pulled on the white shoes. They had a three-inch heel and his calves ached.

The three women lost interest in him as Fiona spoke. "Each stage has options. So if you turn to page 25 for example you'll see the options I have already outlined for her clitty for example."

Elizabeth flipped through the pages and then pushed down on page 25.

Fiona continued. "Clitty decoration is no charge as I'll leave that to you. Hormone therapy is part of a wider physical change and is costed as option 2. Surgery for reconstruction is there as option 3 and broken down into breast and clitty."

Elizabeth studied the page. "Thanks, Fiona I'll look at this document and let you know. It's very comprehensive and I can see you have lots of experience in this area."

"Yes," agreed Fiona. "Almost twenty-five years of male improvement. I also have a feminisation school where I teach nasty males to become good girls."

Elizabeth stood to give the hint that the meeting was over. Clara followed her and Fiona stood. "Before I leave I want to invite you to our club."

"What club would that be?" asked Elizabeth.

"It's an invitation-only club for ladies to relax and enjoy themselves. We are served by submissive girlies such as the one you have here. The girlies are there for our pleasure and entertainment and to serve us. The only rule is that anything goes for the ladies and the girlies do as they're told. It's held at a secret location but if you're interested I'll send you an invite by email. And please feel free to bring Clara and Patty. It will be good for Patty to be subjected to a wider dominant female environment. You can meet other ladies with your interests and your status in society. All our members are highly successful ladies, like you. I'm sure you'll get some ideas and opinions from others about which parts of my proposal you wish to take. Your friend Melissa is a member, of course."

Elizabeth's eyebrows raised. "Yes, that sounds wonderful, do send me the details Fiona. We'd love to come to your ladies' club. It sounds wonderful."

"I'll send you the details as soon as I get back to the office at my feminisation school."

"I look forward to it." Elizabeth smiled and turned to

Patrick, her lips parted like a shark about to eat its next meal. He didn't like the sound of that club or Elizabeth's enthusiasm for it.

Chapter 14 - The new journey begins

Patrick stood in the damp, wide avenue. The earlier rainstorm threatened to resume at any moment. Elizabeth held a leather leash attached to his collar. It was late and a brisk wind blew at his tiny skirt and brushed a shard of long platinum blond hair across his cheek.

Even with the light makeup, his face and body retained a certain masculinity. He was relieved that there were no pedestrians around to see him. A few large cars with resident stickers on their windscreens were parked along the street. Thick clouds obscured the night stars and the area was bathed in a dirty orange by the glare from the city's street lights.

Chilly air licked at his balls and penis beneath his five-inch long white chiffon skirt. The end of his penis was no more than a quarter of an inch from the bottom of the skirt. He yearned to get out of the open street and away from the risk of exposure. His skirt covered his penis for now. He had to hope that where they were going would be cool

Elizabeth had told him they were going to Fiona Allerton's ladies' club in west London. He had received no other explanation from his wife about what to expect. Elizabeth, Clara and her sister Charlotte had had a fun time dressing him up in preparation for the evening. They had giggled and played around before settling on his outfit. Clara had suggested the collar that chaffed around his neck. His black fishnet stockings provided little protection from the chill. The large diamond-shaped areas exposed smooth flesh between the fine netting. He snuggled his head into his shoulders. He was thankful for his thick rich hair which covered his neck and much of his face. His pink padded jacket formed a barrier against the windy chill around his torso.

Elizabeth and Charlotte stood next to him chatting. Elizabeth played with the loop of his leash absent-mindedly. His eyes flitted around the street nervously in the silence. Clara had dropped them off where they now waited. She had driven off to find a parking spot in one of the many smaller side streets that spun off the road. Lights peeked out from blinds and thick curtains of the large houses lining both sides of the street. A flag fluttered from a small white pole above a door. It was an Arabic nation's consulate.

They heard the clip of Clara's heels echoing from the white exterior walls of the high elegant houses before she appeared. Clara joined them and rubbed her hands together, a mix of the chill and the anticipation. They set off along the street, Elizabeth tugged at Patrick's leash. It was as if he were a pet as she called out, *"Come on girl"*. He didn't feel as loved as pets do.

They walked along the row of silent terraced houses. At the end of the street, a line of black London taxis and red double-decker buses ground on. Nothing turned down this road. Elizabeth stopped in front of a set of steps up to a solid black door. The number 69 in black metallic letters was attached to the door above a wide brass letterbox. Tall sash windows had wooden shutters behind them, closed against the night.

A smaller set of concrete steps led down to a basement area. At one time, it would have been the servant quarters but now it was blocked off by a high black metal grill. Lights shone onto a small patio from the uncovered basement windows.

Elizabeth scrolled through the address on her phone then back up at the street number. She surveyed the area around her as if that would help her decide. Patrick hoped this was their destination. The sooner he was off the street the better.

Chapter 15 – Girl training

Elizabeth accepted Fiona Allerton's feminisation proposal. For the previous three weeks, she followed Fiona's instructions to the letter. Fiona Allerton's proposal said that Patrick should be dressed rather than naked. The dress style was exceptionally feminine: mini skirts and dresses with lots of feminine pleats and frills. He wore the clothing with equanimity, deciding that it was better than being naked. He realised too that he was beginning to enjoy female clothing.

Fiona visited three times a week for two-hour sessions to instruct him in being feminine – walking, sitting and mannerisms. Fiona remained on her feet for the entire session while tapping a cane against the side of her leg.

She made other changes to his clothing. She locked him in six-inch heels. The shoe straps around his ankles were held in place with small chrome heart-shaped padlocks. He walked on bent-up toes. His toes and leg muscles had ached terribly at first. He was becoming accustomed to the acute angle now. His calves ached less and less. His toe tendons appeared to have shortened. He noticed his leg muscles were more defined; that wasn't so bad. It was uncomfortable to walk in bare feet since Fiona had begun his training. He was only permitted out of his six-inch heels to have a shower. He even had to sleep in them. His feet were slowly being re-shaped.

They trudged up the wide steps to the front door. The gloss black door was a solid panelled door, double width. A square grey security pad was set on the wall at shoulder height to the right of the door. A small LED light glowed red. A metallic speaker in a box sat next to the pad with a thick black plastic button. Above the door, two black security cameras blinked at them like watching vultures.

Elizabeth pressed the black button and waited as a warbling ringing sound came from the tinny speaker. Patrick felt exposed at the top of the steps. His tiny skirt contrasted with Elizabeth and Charlotte's elegant dresses and Clara's smart wide grey trousers. The ringing sound stopped and a female voice answered with a single, *'Yes'*.

"Elizabeth Remington, two guests and a girl."

Patrick processed the word girl with despair. A low buzzing like an angry wasp trying to escape sounded out from the door with the sound of a catch releasing. Elizabeth pushed against the door. A car passed, its headlamps swept over them like searchlights. The door swung open into a small lobby. A light flickered and flashed on, activated by a hidden motion detector.

They bundled through the door which swung shut behind them. The floor was a matrix of small black and white diamond tiles. The walls and ceiling were plain matt white. An ornate coving and a picture rail ran along the top of the wall. Their bubbly chatter fell away, replaced by an eeriness in the harsh light of the corridor. The low whine of a cello bounced towards them from somewhere in the building, too faint to make out any tune.

A second door faced them as if the entrance was an airlock. It was white and panelled. Another camera was set above the door, watching them. There was no door handle, another grey swipe pad sat on the wall. A brass metal button was set on the wall to its right. Soft cello music rose in the background. The three ladies said nothing. Patrick knew not to speak. A minute or two passed then the sound of a metal bar sliding in a groove. A key slid into the door from the other side.

 The door shuddered and shook for a moment, stiff and heavy. It swished open on smooth hinges. They walked through the threshold into a long hall. Patrick's first impression was of the entrance passage for a stately home from a TV series. Chandelier lights threw a jewelled white light from the ceiling. A white-stockinged knee protruded from behind the door. Whoever had opened the door was curtseying to them.

 The door slammed behind them with a firm clunk. A bolt slid firm and a key turned. Patrick blinked, his eyes adapting to the duller lighting. A tall well-built person got up from the deep curtsey and faced them. An angular head with blond hair in two long side ponytails. Large pink ribbons tied in bows tumbled over large protruding ears with dangling earrings. The man was in a powder-pink maid's dress pushed out by layers of stiff ruffled petticoats. He flashed black false eyelashes against a square face.

"Please follow me, ladies, Mistresses Allerton and Ademola are expecting you." He curtsied again and stepped down the corridor in an ungainly gait in high stiletto heels.

Embossed grey-flecked wallpaper lined the walls. They passed a double-width wooden staircase. It swept up to the next floor and down to an unseen basement area. The cello music was louder now and wafted up from the stairs. A cocktail of voices hummed and merged with the music below. The maid stopped at the end of the corridor and knocked on an internal door. A voice called out from the other side for them to enter. It was Fiona Allerton. The sissy maid opened the door and stepped back, eyes to the floor. Elizabeth, Clara and Charlotte entered. Patrick followed them in at the rear.

The room was a large brightly-lit modern office with folding doors along the entire back wall. A green swath of grass and bushes outside were lit by floor lights. The office had a contemporary corporate style completely different to the entrance hall. Two dark-wood desks were set at right angles to each other. High-backed corporate-style leather chairs were tucked in behind them. The desks glinted with a dull shine.

Fiona Allerton waited in front of one of the desks. She beamed and marched over to Elizabeth. They kissed on both cheeks and she then air-kissed Clara and Charlotte. Her eyes flicked to Patrick who remembered to curtsey. Fiona had her hair pulled back and stacked up in a bun. A silver needle held it up and a vibrant blue dress hugged her tall frame. She was over six feet tall in her heels.

Another lady sat on the front edge of the other desk. A long uncovered dark leg crossed over the other, her hands rested on either side on the desktop. This lady watched the greetings with a cool detachment through glacial-blue eyes. She wore a black suit jacket, as if expecting a business meeting. Her matching pencil skirt rested above her smooth knees.

Patrick curtsied to her as her eyes flowed over him. They settled on his skirt. He pulled at the hem realising the end of his penis was showing as it had expanded in the warm internal air. He lowered the skirt further on his hips, the waistband now sitting across his pubic hairline. He couldn't pull it down any further. His penis was going to show if it grew any further.

There was little more he could do except hope it was chillier elsewhere. Wherever it was they were.

Fiona introduced the lady with the blue eyes: Aretta Ademola. Aretta stood up and strode over to Elizabeth and then Clara and Charlotte. She shook hands with each of the ladies; her talon-like red nails inter-twined with their fingers. The air of a business meeting persisted. Aretta moved over to Patrick and circled him like a panther. Her tall heels sank into the plush dark blue carpet. Aretta was four inches taller than Patrick, her long hair black and shiny like a raven's feathers. Her ebony skin was blemish and wrinkle-free as if it had been sandblasted smooth.

"What do we have here then?" She stopped, facing Patrick. She gave out a long purr and licked her lips. The prowling panther seemed stronger and more dangerous now. His body became hot and sticky. Aretta rocked back on her heels as if ready to pounce on him.

"This is Patricia, or Patty. Or you can call her Girl," said Elizabeth.

"And she's yours?" Aretta continued to stare at Patrick.

"Yes, she's mine," answered Elizabeth.

"I want to ask your permission to use your property."

"You may borrow her for whatever you have in mind."

Aretta narrowed her eyes and Patrick went from hot to a deep chill. Something told him that whatever Aretta had in mind for him would be uncomfortable.

Chapter 16 – Introductions

"Has anyone ever taken her? I get the feeling she's a virgin, new to this." Aretta said.

"Yes, she's new to femininity and submission. She's in training but needs a good introduction to her future." Elizabeth leant on a chair, relaxed and happy to hand Patrick over.

Aretta was close to Patrick's face. He shuddered. Aretta had no warmth. He saw only a deep pool of darkness in her cold eyes and across her drawn mouth. Aretta lifted the front of his skirt and spat on his penis. He flinched back in shock as her saliva oozed off. He moved a hand to wipe it away. Aretta slapped his fingers away. She put her face closer to his, an inch away. Elizabeth, Clara and Charlotte watched, transfixed by Aretta.

"Open your mouth wide and put your tongue out," said Aretta.

Patrick's wide unblinking eyes flitted to Elizabeth,

pleading in silence. Elizabeth was fascinated by the unfolding show. She was not going to help; he should have known. He opened his mouth and put his tongue out. He became worried she would hurt his tongue. She spat again and her saliva slapped on his tongue. She spat in his eyes.

"Swallow my spit, girl and then you can thank me for condescending to allow you to taste some of my body fluid."

Patrick shuddered and pulled his tongue back into his mouth. He swallowed and her warm saliva slid down his throat. His hands twitched by his side, he wanted to wipe away her spit drooling down his nose. Aretta's cold eyes told him that would be a bad idea. She gazed deep and dark. Her minty breath gusted into his face, her musky smell invaded his senses. She picked up the loose leash Elizabeth had left to swing by his side.

"I can do anything, Elizabeth?" Aretta spoke without removing her eyes from Patrick. He stared down to the floor.

"She's all yours, Aretta," Elizabeth replied. "Do as you please."

"Excellent, it's been a while since I had a virgin." Aretta's almost-perfect BBC English enunciation had the faint hint of an accent. He couldn't place it. African maybe? Aretta pulled hard on his leash, choking him. He coughed as Aretta pulled him to her desk. There was a set of four pieces of A4 paper held together in the corner by a lime-green paper clip. The top sheet had a series of lines and under that his male name, Patrick Hayley. Two names were written under his and beneath the word, witnesses: Aretta Ademola and Fiona Allerton's names had a series of dotted lines next to them. A slim silver pen lay by the paper.

"Sign this document, girl." Aretta indicated the place for Patrick to sign with a long slim dark finger.

Patrick delayed, he didn't know what she wanted him to sign for.

Elizabeth spotted his hesitation. "It's the membership for the club. You need to apply and be sponsored by two members. In this case, Fiona and Aretta. Sign it and we can go in."

An alarm rang in his head. Something wasn't right. He didn't trust them. It was not a form but a contract of some kind. "Sorry, Ms Remington, but it says witnesses, not sponsors."

"It's the same thing. Sign it, stupid girl, and hurry up. We're getting fed up waiting as you dither."

Aretta placed the pen on the line for his signature. He was being pushed into signing something he did not understand. The document's papers were hidden below the one Aretta had told him to sign. He took the pen and lifted the top piece of paper. He scanned the words which were legalese. Aretta slammed her hand down to put the top sheet back down. She slapped him across the cheek. "Sign it."

He was not going to get to look. It might have been a membership form. The word *witness* worried him. That was usually for a contract but he had no choice. He would have to sign or face punishment. He hated conflict. He signed it to end the stand-off; it was the easiest option for a quiet life. A sense of unease continued to pervade his mind. Aretta pulled on his leash and led Patrick out of the office to the stairs. He followed behind, marvelling at her physique and the way she glided. She was tall and toned and moved like an African gazelle.

Aretta glided down the stairs pulling him with her. He held

on to the bannister for balance, his heels slipping on the smooth stair tiles. They descended the wide circular stairs. The classical music became louder as they approached the basement. The cello was joined by a violin.

At the bottom of the stairs, a small lobby area led to wooden-framed glass double doors. The subdued light beyond the doors lit a massive open room with bookcases and luxurious furniture. Women of all ages sat in chairs reading, chatting and taking drinks. Up-lighters threw soft lighting against the light walls. Frosted glass at the top of the walls glowed orange from the street lights outside.

Several girls milled around serving, some appeared bigger than most of the women there and dressed in maid's dresses. Two girls stood upright waiting against a wall. A set of fingers clicked and one of them jolted straight and shot over to ask what they wanted.

Aretta pushed open the doors and now it was obvious that the servers were feminised males. They wore identical black uniform dresses. White embroidery ran around the hem and sleeves. The servers had small white aprons with frilled edges and wore white French-maid caps. All wore four-inch high-heeled black sandals and patterned black stockings. The real women were all dressed in style.

Patrick followed Aretta through the enormous room. On seeing Aretta, several of the maids curtsied. She stopped for a moment and soaked up their respect as Patrick waited behind her. His leash remained wrapped tightly around her wrist. To his left, two elegantly dressed young ladies played the cello and violin on a tiny stage. A grand piano sat moodily by them.

Aretta pulled on his leash and led him away from the musicians. One side of the room was set out with round tables and chairs, like an elegant French café. Several women were taking snacks. Some of the women had feminised males sitting at their feet. These males were dressed in a variety of dresses and skirts. Other feminised males stood to attention as their ladies chatted, ate nibbles and drank.

All the males had collars around their necks. Leashes similar to Patrick's hung from several. Male maids served drinks and food and took orders. No one was interested in him as Aretta generated curtsies from the males as they passed through. Aretta stopped to chat with some females.

Patrick recognised one lady she was talking to, a well-known TV news presenter. Patrick froze with surprise to see she was with a senior female member of the government; a male in a short skirt sat by her feet, head down. She fed him bits of bread broken off from a sandwich as if he was a pet.

Patrick's scanned the room. He saw female sports stars, businesswomen and female politicians. It was full of female high achievers. He saw a senior female government leader in deep discussion with a well-known female politician from the USA and the female prime minister of a Scandinavian country. He couldn't remember which country but her husband was on a leash sitting by her feet.

Aretta said her goodbyes and dragged an open-mouthed Patrick to the end of the room. A bar area served alcohol, tea and coffee and stretched along the back wall. Tall indoor plants screened off the bar. Two male maids served drinks while other maids delivered them to ladies in the bar or took them into the main area.

Aretta passed through another set of double doors by the

bar which led into a small lobby. This area was darker with indoor plants scattered around the walls. Four plain doors fed off from this lobby. Aretta pushed through into the first room. A low light emanated from wall lights. Aretta gave his leash to a young woman standing inside the windowless room.

"Wait," she said to Patrick.

His eyes adjusted to the low light. The young woman holding his leash wore a pretty red skater dress. Her shoulder-length hair was red and streaked with light blue. She pushed him on the top of his head. She wanted him to sit on the floor. It suited him as his tiny skirt flared out around his thighs covering his still flaccid penis.

His attention was drawn to two attractive women giggling hysterically. Their similar tight black miniskirts were wrapped tight around their thighs. Volumes of bleach-blond hair flowed around their faces and down their backs. Two naked males lay on the floor at their feet. They were in a sixty-nine position sucking on each other's erect penises. One looked plaintively at the women as if to ask permission to stop. Patrick's mouth dropped as he saw the man's body jerk as he orgasmed into the mouth of the other. The two women screamed in delight, clapping with joy.

Aretta returned and dragged him to an area with a bench padded with black leather. She had changed. She was now dressed in black leather trousers and a leather vest. The clothing fitted her like a second skin and her arms rippled with toned muscle. His eyes widened at the sight of an enormous rubber cock strapped to her waist. It stuck out from her groin like a real erection.

"You enjoyed seeing those sissies giving each other a blow job? Good. Suck on this."

He could do that, it wasn't the end of the world to suck on a false cock. It might have been much worse. He put his lips around the cock, an effigy of a black male's erection. Eight inches of solid rubber.

"Good girl," murmured Aretta as he sucked.

The others in the room were not watching which suited Patrick. Aretta pulled his head away from her strap-on by his long bleach-blond hair.

"Turn around, girl," she said.

Aretta placed his chest flat on the bench, his stomach rested on the end, his legs wide apart on either side. Aretta pulled his skirt up onto the small of his back exposing his bare bum. The girl in the red skater skirt wandered over with a bored expression. A blunt rubber or plastic object touched his bum cheeks. It was Aretta's strap-on cock. This was not good, he thought.

Chapter 17 - Taken behind

"This girl's mistress has told me she is a virgin. She's never been pegged before. You will be witness to a rare event: the breaking of a virgin."

Patrick lifted his head. The two mini-skirted ladies had finished with their show and came to watch Aretta. He didn't know what Aretta was talking about. What did pegged mean?

A chill bit at his bum hole. It was not unpleasant. He felt a smooth object push against his sphincter muscles, probing but not entering. He twisted his neck to try to see what Aretta was doing. She stood behind him, resting her weight on a strap-on penis that dug into his bum hole. He did not like what was threatened and he did not like people watching him.

He thought again about the two men giving each other blowjobs and shuddered. The women here seemed to believe there were no limits. A surge of panic rushed into his throat. He prayed that Aretta was not going to put that lump of silicone inside him.

The end of Aretta's strap-on erection circled again, threatening but not entering. Aretta whispered in his ear, telling him to relax, she wasn't going to hurt him. As long as he accepted his fate. The pain would only come if he didn't embrace what was about to happen. He had to surrender and enjoy the moment.

The young lady in the red dress began to beat a slow handclap. The two other ladies took up the rhythm. The two naked men looked up from the floor, grateful that someone else was the focus of attention.

Aretta's rubberised cock drew more invisible circles around his twitching anus. Patrick was taut with anticipation. She homed in and it entered a little. She withdrew it again, as if testing him for flexibility. She cooed out an instruction, "*Relax, enjoy.*" He tightened his whole body involuntarily. He didn't want an object in his bum.

Aretta probed again, then pushed the silicone penis an inch inside him. He let out a sharp "ugh" sound from his constricted throat. His mouth went dry. Aretta giggled. She was teasing and testing him. She pushed the artificial penis head further inside him. A pang of intense pleasure and discomfort hit him as his muscles stretched and fought back. He tried to resist the foreign element inside him.

He waited for Aretta to withdraw the strap-on again. She kept it in, at least two inches inside him. She waited a moment, letting him become used to the sensation of a cock inside him. Then she eased it in and pleasure lapped in his stomach like waves against a sandy beach. His penis jerked to life at the new deep eroticism. He tried to hold it back. This was wrong, he told himself.

Aretta received advice from one of her three-women audience, *"Push it in all the way."* Laughter. He closed his eyes as he felt the fake penis slide in further, another half an inch. His insides expanded to take it, the shape of the penis head palpable against his inner rectum. A part of his brain screamed more, the other half shouted, no.

He wiped away the thought of wanting it with self-disgust. But he was enjoying it. That wasn't right. He had never been interested in anal play before and he didn't want to now. Or did he? *Wasn't that a gay thing*? He wasn't gay. *Or was he?*

He was confused. He was being pushed into something new, awful and fascinating. Another new reality confronted him.

Aretta circled her hips to circle and the rubber penis circled inside him, widening his passage, preparing the way. Pain, ecstasy and a nascent headache throbbed. The three women clapped a beat. Then a searing shaft of pain. Aretta's penis shot in and the warm leather of her waist strap hit his bum cheeks with a dull slap.

He yelped like a wounded hyena as pain hit him combined with extreme euphoria. Sweat dripped from his forehead and onto the floor. He felt the rubber cock inside him withdraw with a slow drag. It was almost out when Aretta shoved back in all the way, hard and straight like an underground train thundering on the tracks. There was less pain this time. His muscles stretched to allow her in; he surrendered.

This time, the penis hit something deep inside him. Aretta kept it deep inside him. Billows of intense orgasmic pleasure blew through his body. His erection stiffened and he came without warning. His slimy discharge spurted under his stomach and dripped from the bench. He sunk his chest into the bench and relief coursed through him.

For a few moments, he soaked up the pleasure and forgot where he was. A sensual gratification. Then the horror of the ignominy. He had just been taken in the bum and cum for an audience.

Aretta withdrew the imitation penis and spoke to the red-dressed girl. "Spank her would you, Janice, and then get her to clean up her mess." Aretta walked away. She removed the strap-on while muttering about how she loved taking virgins.

The girl in the red skater dress tied his hands around the bench. He hadn't recovered from the intense orgasm and gave in weakly. Janice flexed a thin cane in her hands like a schoolmistress about to punish an errant pupil. Janice disappeared from his eye line.

A swish of air preceded a sharp stinging pain against the cheeks of his bum. He squealed. Another swish and more intense stinging pain. The cane rained on his bottom again and again, *swish-slap, swish-slap*. It stopped. The gentle touch of a warm hand rubbed against the sore welts on his skin. A soothing kindness after the cruelty. His bum cheeks throbbed and pulsed. Janice untied him. He passed his freed hands over thin raised welts.

He pushed himself up, feeling stupid. Aretta returned and held out a roll of paper kitchen towels and a cleaning spray. Patrick took it and cleaned up his mess on the floor under the watchful glare of the red-haired girl. Patrick spent a while over-cleaning the floor. He wanted to use the time to recover. Another pair of feet stopped by him. Black stiletto heels filled his vision. Fiona Allerton peered down at him over the top of her glasses.

"I want you to clean your mess off the bench before it dries," she said.

He got onto his knees and sprayed cleaning fluid into a fresh piece of the kitchen paper roll he had torn off.

"Oh no you don't, Patty. Put that down." Her hands were on her hips.

He didn't understand how he could clean the bench without the kitchen roll.

As if reading his mind, she said, "You'll lick it up with your tongue and swallow it. Like a slutty girl does. Get on with it."

Patrick stared at her. She couldn't be serious. She glared back at him, she was deadly serious. His slimy cum was smeared over the leather bench and he shivered as the salty damp smell rose up. A small acidic heave entered his throat and he fought it back down. Fiona indicated that he start. He dropped his head to the bench, the salty damp smell mingled with the odour of warm leather. He flicked his tongue out and caught a blob of the cold semen. A slimy phlegm taste oozed in his mouth. He swallowed, shuddered and it slipped down his throat like a rancid oyster.

A whack on his sore bottom urged him to hurry. He cleared the bench with his tongue rapidly. He shivered at each mouthful of cold slimy semen. A sick taste stuck in the back of his mouth He finished and stood. He threw the screwed-up towel away in a large bin in the corner of the room and left the cleaning spray on the floor. He returned to the waiting Fiona Allerton.

"Aren't we forgetting something?" Her imperious gave fixed him over her glasses.

Patrick shuddered. He had the idea it was a shudder of

delight at her manner. But that was too weird. He curtsied.

"That's better. Good girl. Now follow me." She took the leash hanging from his collar and spun around gracefully as if she were a ballerina. "We have a few more changes to make to you. To make you into a much better girl."

The words were like a thump in his chest. *What more could they do to him?*

Chapter 18 – And there's more

Patrick scampered behind Fiona and back into the dimly-lit lobby. There was a faint sound of light piano music.

Fiona led Patrick to the far door and they went through it. The room looked like a medical room. The plain emulsioned walls were flat white and white cupboards ran around the room. There was a metal sink and draining board in the centre of the work surface.

A single metal-framed medical bed stood in the middle of the room. It had a metal headboard and two side bars which had been lowered. The bed was at waist height.

Fiona motioned with her cane for Patrick to sit on the edge of the bed. Aretta Ademola sat in one corner in a plastic chair. Elizabeth stood next to her.

"What are you going to do, Mistress?" Patrick asked.

Fiona stood erect, her legs apart like a gunslinger. She tapped her cane in a cupped hand. Before he could repeat the question, the door to the room swung open. A young lady strode in with a calm business-like manner. She had short blond hair, flat shoes and a white overcoat like a laboratory technician. Her unmade-up face was pasty and bored.

She carried a large leather bag slung over one of her narrow shoulders. She placed the bag at Patrick's feet and pulled a small silver staple gun-like device from inside. She got up and leant forward, pushing his hair back from his ears in a more delicate fashion than her expression had threatened. She clipped the staple gun on his lobe and pushed hard before he could react. He winced at the sharp pain and his fingers shot to his ear to explore. She stapled his other earlobe. Another jolt of pain shot through him.

"A little oversight corrected," Fiona said.

A warm damp feeling met his touch. And cold thin metal. He inspected his fingertips. A little blood was smeared on his fingers. She had pierced earrings into his earlobes. He sighed. They had done so much to him, this was one more hurdle to accept.

"Would you like to see your earrings, Miss?"

Miss? The young lady had called him Miss. He pushed her

comment away from his mind, it was no worse than all the other names he was being called. It was a good deal more polite than being called Girl.

He nodded, he had a morbid desire to see the one more nail in the coffin of his masculinity.

The young lady took a small circular make-up mirror from one of her white jacket pockets. She held it up. He turned his head from side to side. Light golden earrings dangled two inches from his lobes. They were pretty, he had to admit. He kept his face passive, not wanting to give the watching women any satisfaction. He flicked his head again to make them jangle.

He fidgeted on his chair, the feeling of something more about to happen floating over him. This was not all about earrings, he guessed that was the appetiser. He wondered what the main course was going to be. His wife sauntered over to him. The feeling of foreboding rose. Elizabeth paced for a few moments, like a brooding lioness.

"Patty, Patty, Patty. What am I going to do with you?" She paced back and forth.

Patrick was not sure if the question was rhetorical or if she expected an answer.

Elizabeth answered his silent question. "You're so passive. I selected you for your lack of endeavour and drive as well as your slim feminine appearance." She paused. "I'd hoped for a little more fight. I enjoyed you running away to my friend Melissa's. That was amusing and I thought that was the beginning of some pushback. The trouble is you haven't pushed back again. I wanted your feminisation to be a bit more of a challenge. That would make it more fun. I'm wondering if you're not enjoying being a girl a little too much. The truth is that I suspect that as long as you are getting fed, have a warm room to live in and no responsibility then you don't care."

Elizabeth pursed her lips in thought. Patrick said nothing but had to admit that his shrewd wife had a point. He would rather not be here at this women's club be humiliated. On balance, he had settled into what Elizabeth what doing as he preferred to go along with someone else's ideas. He had a free place to live, free food and he didn't have to worry about where his next penny was coming from. That advantage trumped most things Elizabeth could do to him. But there was one more aspect to it. Being feminised and pretty had a strange unexpected attraction.

Elizabeth stopped her pacing. "I wanted a husband to control and feminise. But I hadn't planned to make you suffer initially. Well not too much. I chose you as I knew you'd be passive and you'd go along with my needs in return for a quiet comfortable life. You would have had a very comfortable stress-free life as a pretty feminised husband. If you hadn't tried to double-cross me."

Patrick was tired of hearing this. Elizabeth certainly bore a grudge.

Elizabeth took a breath, then launched into the next part of her tirade. "The trouble is, you accepted it. You even ejaculated when Aretta pegged you. That was supposed to be a humiliating punishment. A show of your subjugation. And you enjoyed it."

Patrick had no idea where Elizabeth's rant was going. He hoped she felt better once it was all out. That was not going to happen. Once she had got her teeth into something she would never let go. She was leading to something more, that was clear.

"So," Elizabeth added. "I've made you a cuckold, put you in schoolgirl clothes, humiliated you and had you pegged and caned. You've taken every punch I've thrown at you. Now it's time to ramp things up a whole lot more. Everything I've done to you can be reversed. However, Fiona's proposal included some physical changes that would be irreversible. I've decided to adopt Fiona's proposal and make permanent changes. I don't want you to be able to revert to being a male. I want you to remain as a girl with no going back. In addition, she suggested you find work in a role that is suitable for an unqualified girl. A typist or a waitress for example. I like that idea.

Patrick flinched. *Permanent changes? Work?* This didn't sound good at all. Elizabeth called the young lady in the lab coat over. Her bored expression hadn't changed one iota at hearing Elizabeth's speech. She waited by Elizabeth.

"So two things are going to happen to you, Patty. Firstly work. Fiona said that you need to get a real job. A job that is associated with a girl. Not a pretend one at my office where you can flounce around in your little skirts and the girls can play with you. No, you're going to have to earn money to start contributing to my household. You will be working for Fiona but you won't be working at her feminisation school. You'll be working in the big wide world as a girl. She won't be paying you much so you'll need to earn your tips. You have no skills so an unskilled job suits you."

Patrick sat up straight. That sounded like real work. He had never had to do real work before. He didn't like the sound of this. Elizabeth's face broke into a smile at seeing his displeasure.

"I see that finally, you're not happy. Good. You'll find out next week what your new job will be." Elizabeth was in her stride now. She paced the floor again, this time with her confidence up. "Secondly, we're going to make some major changes to your feminisation. These changes will be permanent, as I said. And *very* feminine." She pointed at the girl in the lab coat. "This nice young lady will be starting that process in a few minutes. What she will do is only the start.

But we have to start somewhere if we want you to be a *proper girl.*"

Patrick's mouth dropped open. *A proper girl?* He tried to get off the bed. Elizabeth moved her hand to his chest and stopped him. "Ms Remington," he said. A tone of panic in his voice. "What are you going to do to me? Please don't do anything permanent. I've served my punishment."

"More reaction, some fight back. Excellent. You're going to be so pretty when I've finished with you. Your mother, God rest her soul, won't even recognise you by the time we've finished with you."

Chapter 19 – Feminised and pretty sore

It was as if he'd been attacked by a thousand wasps. His legs, chest, under his arms, his balls and penis, his eyes and eyelids and his cheeks. His body was a mass of red sore spots. His eyes were sore, his lips swollen. The young lady worked on him all night. She had been very thorough.

He lay on his bed in his small plain bedroom unable to sleep from the stinging and skin irritation. Elizabeth had kept his six-inch heels locked to his feet and he was still wrapped in the white gown the lab technician lady had put on him. She had used electrolysis on his entire body. She had even removed his eyebrows. The only hair remaining below his neck was a perfect triangle of hair above his penis. A perfect facsimile of a female's pubic shape.

She had told him his body hair was unlikely to ever grow back. Elizabeth had carried out her threat. Permanent change. But she had done more. The lady had tattooed his face, eyelids and eyebrows with permanent makeup.

She had also worked with the tattoo gun on his penis and stomach. That had stung the most. They hadn't let him see what she had done. Elizabeth had thought it very amusing, whatever it was. He hadn't yet seen his new face either. Elizabeth, Charlotte and Clara had giggled all the way back home. Charlotte had kept looking into his face and bursting into hysterical laughter. Once home, they had taken him to bed. He had fallen asleep instantly.

He had lain on the bed for around forty-five minutes after waking, too dozy to move. It was light. He pushed himself up and the clock by his bed said 01.31 pm. His arms were hairless and blotchy, tiny red circles burned where the hairs had been removed. He sat up and put his feet on the floor. Pink nail varnish glistened from his toenails.

He pushed himself to his feet and balanced on the heels, swaying left and then right in his weakness. He needed to see what they had done to him. He pulled the gown around his body and staggered over to the mirror on his wardrobe. He put his face close up to the glass. He staggered back on his heels like a drunken stilt-walker at what he saw. A beaten-up face reflected back at him. He swayed and moved in close again.

His brows were thin and arched. His eyelids were a swollen dusky grey. A thin black line traced out his eyes on his upper and lower lids. The tattoos were exactly like eyeliner and mascara. A permanent tattoo lip-liner accentuated the lip filler the technician had injected. He had a pout like a gasping fish. She had said it would go down in a day or so and be more natural. How natural was a matter of opinion, he thought.

He inspected his eyes again. Something was odd. There was the tattooed eyeliner in a flick at the outside corner of each of his eyes. It was a Latina flick, like a poor copy of Amy Winehouse. For a moment, his head swam in blackness as if he might pass out. He shook his head. He stared again. Each time, something new struck him. His lashes were longer. Much longer. She had implanted lashes top and bottom.

Elizabeth had gone too far this time. He stared again. His face was swollen. He would have to wait until the swelling went down. He hoped it wouldn't be as bad as it seemed now. He didn't know what to think, his mind was scrambled. He needed to sleep a little more. The young technician lady had worked on him all night.

His white gown fell open as he staggered across to his bed. He didn't care. He threw himself onto the bed and rested his head on the headboard. He was too tired to think straight. He let the dressing gown fall away, exposing his nudity. His eyes flowed down his smooth clear chest. The trim triangle of dark pubic hair was raised on a female-style mount.

He sat up with a start. The bored-looking technician girl had injected something there and it had swollen up like a woman's mount. There was also something black written across his stomach and down the length of his penis. His tired eyes refused to focus.

He squinted and rubbed his eyes. He brushed away at the black markings on his stomach as if they were dust or fluff. They were raised and swollen. It was another tattoo. He focused his tired eyes on his stomach. There were two rows of lettering, an inch above the top of his triangular pubic mount. He remembered the stinging pain when the young lady had tattooed his stomach. His eyes widened as he interpreted the upside-down letters.

This SLUT is the property of
Elizabeth Remington

"No," he screamed. It can't be permanent, he thought. Even Elizabeth wouldn't have done that to him. He licked his fingers and rubbed. His stomach skin was sore. Heat flowed through his veins, his temples throbbed. He rubbed again. It had to be henna, it had to be. But it was raised and he remembered the tattoo needle working on his skin. There was more tattooing on his penis. The lettering ran from the base of his penis to his foreskin:

C

L

I

T

T

Y

Blood rushed into his temples. Now he was angry. She had tattooed the word clitty onto his penis. How dare she?

He heard voices downstairs, Elizabeth's booming voice above the others. He got up and wrapped the gown around himself. He stomped out of his bedroom and to the top of the stairs. His head was tight and heavy, as if it had a vice around it. He needed to sort this out with Elizabeth. She'd gone too far this time.

She had wanted to goad him, to make him angry. Now she had succeeded. How could she have him tattooed with those terrible words? This was abuse. His mind whirled, this may be his chance, his reason to get a divorce. It wasn't how he had wanted it but she had given him an opening. He would be free and rich. A huge settlement for her abuse. Elizabeth had overplayed her hand.

He stomped downstairs. A new sense of balance came over him as he descended in his locked-on high heels. While he was at it, he would complain about her locking the shoes on him.

Yes, he had her now, she had gone too far. It had to be illegal to have him tattooed without his consent. Physical abuse, domestic violence against a vulnerable husband. Yes, that was his angle.

As he continued down the stairs, he imagined she would settle out of court. She would have to otherwise it would be bad for her business. A high-profile court case was not what she would want. It was odd though, Elizabeth was usually so calculated. It didn't matter, everyone made mistakes. Now she had made a mistake, thinking she was more powerful than she was. A classic error of the rich and powerful.

He heard someone below mention he was coming down. Clara's voice. He got to the bottom of the stairs. He wondered how much she would give him in the settlement: £5 million, £10 million? It was worth the tattoos to get that much. The tattoos were his ticket to freedom and wealth. Besides, with the settlement money he could have them removed. He shuddered at the thought of tattoo removal on his penis.

His anger fell away as he thought about how he had won in the end. A calmness descended over him. He would finally get the freedom and wealth he had planned for by marrying Elizabeth. The old woman Elizabeth. It hadn't been the way he had meant it but the result was the same. He undid his gown. He would confront Elizabeth with the evidence. Show her the mistake she had made, the abuse she had poured on him. *Property of Elizabeth Remington. Clitty. Slut?* He would show her who was a slut.

He swaggered into the kitchen and swung open his gown to display his tattooed stomach and penis. He pointed at his own body for emphasis.

"This is the key to my fortune, Elizabeth. You've gone too far this time. This is abuse. I'm taking you to court."

He froze. Four faces stared back at him. Elizabeth, Clara, Charlotte. And Dan Hunter.

Chapter 20 – Mistress rules

Patrick's anger evaporated and transformed into acute embarrassment. He pulled his gown shut fast, wrapping his arms around his body. Astonishment registered on the four watching faces as they waited for something to happen.

Patrick shuffled and brought himself under control. He told himself to push on with his speech. He was going to explain to Elizabeth how he was leaving her and suing for divorce. Her unacceptable tattooing of his stomach and penis was a step too far. And she would be paying for a hotel room while he found an apartment.

"Elizabeth," he started, He cleared his throat. Elizabeth, Clara, Charlotte and Dan's faces remained impassive. "Elizabeth," he said again, using her first name.

He believed there had been a shift of power away from her allowing him to return to first names. Elizabeth's forehead wrinkled in surprise. Her mouth dropped open.

He puffed himself up. "You've gone too far this time.

You've put permanent writing on my body without my permission. I therefore want an immediate divorce. I'll be citing you for physical abuse. I believe you've seen the proof."

He held the collars of his dressing gown. White and fluffy may not be a lawyer's gown but it did the trick for him at that moment. He waited for her reply.

Elizabeth's smooth forehead creased for a moment. "Show us the tattoos again, Patty."

That wasn't the reaction he'd expected. "Elizabeth, I can't believe you went too far in your quest to get me annoyed. You can't do everything you want," he said feeling some discomfort at her lack of concern.

Elizabeth stepped over to Patrick. She pulled his gown apart and looked over him. He tried to tug it together but Elizabeth's grip prevented him.

"I like them. Don't you?" She turned towards her captive audience and back to Patrick. "It wasn't me who wanted those tattoos, Patty."

Patrick shuffled, discomforted. What was she on about? Dan's eyes glinted in amusement. It was bad enough with the women staring but a man was too much. Especially looking like Mr Toothpaste commercial.

"So who's idea was it, Elizabeth?" he said. "Clara's? Charlotte's? It doesn't matter, they work for you so it's the same. I've got you now — D. I. V. O. R. C. E." That was clever, he thought. "Or you can pay me off in an out-of-court settlement. I don't mind."

Elizabeth chuckled like a little girl. She was not bothered by his threat. He guessed she was too arrogant to realise the trouble she was in. She always got her way and the idea of someone like him getting the better of her was obviously beyond her understanding.

She turned her back on him. "It wasn't Clara or Charlotte's idea either, Patty."

He closed his gown, relieved his penis and awful tattoos were no longer on show to Mr Dan Toothpaste Commercial. He had wanted Elizabeth to squirm at the realisation she had gone too far. He struggled to maintain his confidence. He reminded himself to focus on the payout. "So who's idea was it then, Elizabeth? Dan Hunter's?"

Elizabeth returned to sit with her two assistants. Dan lost interest and wandered to the dining area and fiddled with his mobile phone. Elizabeth glanced at Clara and Charlotte. "Actually, Patty. It was your idea."

What was she talking about? This was not going as he had expected. Now she was making things up. At no time had he given any permission for her to have a tattoo on his stomach and especially not on his penis.

"Don't be silly, Elizabeth. I demand you find me some appropriate clothing and take me to a hotel. It's over."

Elizabeth leant over the kitchen work-surface and picked up some papers. "Remember these, Patty?"

His stomach turned slowly, bile rose in his throat.

She continued. "These are the papers you signed in Fiona and Aretta's office. They state that you request permanent facial make-up and that you have a tattoo on your stomach and penis." She looked up from the papers. "Or should that be clitty?"

Patrick's mouth dried. His tongue stuck to the roof of his mouth. He swiped the papers from his wife and saw his signature scrawled on the papers. Fiona Allerton and Aretta Ademola's signatures as witnesses were alongside it. He flipped through the papers. There was a contract with a tattoo artist called Linda Jones. He should have listened to his inner warning and refused to sign them.

The papers listed the work he had signed up for: permanent make-up and the wording for his stomach and penis tattoos. He dropped the papers on the floor. They floated to the floor, back and forth downwards like sycamore seeds in spring. He had been check-mated again.

Chapter 21 – The men will adore you

The low morning sun peeked through the frosted glass of the front door. Patrick waited in the hallway. He was a few minutes early but he preferred to be ready to avoid problems. His wife made her last-minute calls and arrangements.

Elizabeth lived in a blur of activity and did not need him to get in her way. It was best to wait and give her no excuse to become irritated. It was always him who suffered when she was annoyed. Elizabeth paced the kitchen floor giving instructions to someone on her mobile phone. Clara sat at the dining room table with a laptop typing something.

The swelling on his face had gone down over the past week. Elizabeth said he was ready for the second aspect of his change: a new job. He had dressed in clothing she would approve of. He had got himself ready to avoid any fuss with his wife and her 'wannabe' clone Clara.

He smoothed down his ra-ra miniskirt, three-tiered layers of fine thin cotton. The skirt was a soft powder pink. A pattern of intricate darker pink roses with light green leaves flowed over the material. He was confident that Elizabeth would like him in this skirt and the tight white vest. Light-tan stockings gave his legs a shiny effect. The elasticated hold-up tops peeked below the hem of the tiny ra-ra skirt. C-cup inserts filled out his bra. He had found them in his wardrobe.

He had been correct in his assumption that Elizabeth would be satisfied. She hadn't said anything but the fact she hadn't complained told him had chosen correctly.

Today, Elizabeth had said she was going to allow him to wear panties for hygiene reasons. He wasn't sure what that implied but he was happy to be able to cover up, a little. The thong he wore cut uncomfortably into the crack of his bum. He never understood why women wore them, but at least the string held his butt plug in.

He didn't like the idea of a whole day with a plug as it made him walk in short steps while holding his cheeks together. That was one of the reasons for it he supposed. The front piece of his thong clasped around his penis and balls, squashing them tight. His penis seemed as if it was folded in half. He hoped not to get an erection as the cover would not be sufficient to hold it in. Even without an erection, it was precarious.

Elizabeth glanced at him and muttered, "Good girl." She stared for a brief moment with a perplexed look. It was as if she couldn't believe he was so pretty. He was aware of his extremely feminine appearance as he had studied himself in his bedroom mirror earlier. He had been astonished. He had a beautifully made-up face. His future was permanent smoky-grey eyelids, black mascara and bright red lips. Forever tattooed in place.

His penis shot to an instant erection at the sight of his pretty face and the feel of the fine feminine clothing. He would have spotted someone looking like he now did when he was playing his guitar in the pubs and bars of London. That was a different life now and it seemed so long ago.

He shook his head, delighting in his thick platinum-blond hair. He enjoyed the feel of the fringe on his eyelashes and the hair on his face cheeks. He liked the way it fell over his shoulders and down his neck. He zipped up his pink hip-length padded jacket. His shoulder bag slipped off the glossy surface of his narrow shoulders and he hooked it back on with a thumb. His fingernails were like the long talons of a bird but coated in gloss pink.

He balanced on his six-inch stiletto heels as Clara came to join him. She looked him up and down as Elizabeth's booming voice echoed from the kitchen. She was giving instructions to someone else on her phone.

"You've scrubbed up well Patty. Very pretty." She stood back and inspected him from his high-heeled shoes to his blond hair. "I dare say you'll get a lot of attention from the men today looking like that. You're pretty and your skirt is so short."

He shuddered at her comment. They hadn't told him where they were taking him, just that it was his new job. He was pleased he wasn't going to be working at Elizabeth's offices any more. He didn't want to work anyway and he didn't want to work with a group of women giggling at him all day.

Elizabeth stomped into the hall, jangling her car keys and looking at her watch. "We're late." She saw Patrick as if noticing for the first time. "Well, well, aren't you the pretty one today." She peered at his face. "The permanent make-up has worked well although your face still has something masculine in it." Elizabeth pressed her lips together, her chin to her chest.

Clara spoke. "Maybe we need to consider that medication that Fiona proposed. Hormone therapy."

Patrick's relaxed demeanour stiffened, a reaction spotted by Elizabeth. "Maybe we do, Clara. Oestrogen may be necessary to soften her appearance further. It'll probably affect her little clitty's ability to perform so we could kill two birds with one stone."

Patrick opened his mouth to complain. Elizabeth put a finger on his lips to stop him. "Let's go," she said. "Fiona's waiting for us and we're late."

They journeyed towards outer London with Clara driving. They passed the clogged commuter traffic travelling into the city in the opposite direction. On reaching their destination, Clara parked the car in a small backstreet car park in an upmarket area.

They got out of the car and walked across a humpback stone bridge crossing the river. The water flowed lazily behind the high street. Here the river became a haven for pleasure boats and sunbathing on the grassy banks in summer. Weeping willows lined the grassy banks.

Elizabeth's comments about the possibility of hormones and their effects had made him brood. He also felt stupid he was enjoying his new femininity. He had had to admit to himself he was feminine and pretty and his fears had not been necessary. Being feminine was a wonderful feeling. Once he had become used to the changes, it was an exciting sensation. He seethed a little about the contract he had signed saying he wanted permanent tattooed make-up and lettering. But he had become resigned to his fate.

He still had zero responsibility but free food and bed. He loved his appearance and wearing pretty clothes. What was there not to like? He would have preferred the opportunity to move between male and female appearance but so be it.

His immediate worry was what they had in mind for him as a job. If his wife had wanted him to be the office assistant to a load of women she would have kept him in her company. So why drive him out to the suburbs? And what did Fiona Allerton have for him now?

They walked onto the high street. The street had a mix of the high-street chains seen in any high street across the country. There were several designer clothing shops, traditional pubs and smart restaurants.

Elizabeth led them along the pavement in silence, dodging the throngs of shoppers. The stares from the men and the women fell on Patrick. The men gawped at his exposed legs. The women shot disapproving glances at his exaggerated bimbo style. His appearance was incongruous compared to the business style of his wife and the plain-trouser suited Clara.

They approached a pub. Baskets of colourful flowers hung from hooks above the windows and water dripped from them. A sign announced the name: *The Duchess of Richmond*.

Elizabeth grabbed Patrick's hand and dragged him inside. The faint smell of beer and fried food hit him. A long bar ran along one side with glasses hanging above it. It was a few minutes past eleven and there were two customers. They stared at Patrick. A fire blazed in a large open fire on the other side of the bar. An old brown sofa stood in the bay window and small round wooden tables and chairs filled most of the room. A large blackboard on a wall listed the food and beers they served.

Fiona appeared from nowhere. "Welcome to my little pub-restaurant enterprise." She kissed Elizabeth and Clara on each cheek and glared at Patrick. "Well isn't she the pretty one?"

Patrick looked over the gastropub in horror.

"You'll be working here, Patty," Elizabeth explained.

"What?" he exclaimed.

Elizabeth's face dropped in anger at his lack of respect. She then decided that she didn't have the time. "Yes, Patty. You'll be commuting here every day by train and working here full-time as a barmaid and a waitress."

Patrick's mouth dropped open. Fiona Allerton reached down and touched his skirt between two fingers and rubbed. "Very pretty." You can wear this for work, it's perfect. We need a pretty sexy waitress to keep our mostly male guests happy."

Elizabeth smiled. "I will leave her with you, Fiona."

"Yes of course, Elizabeth. I'll be leaving soon too as I have a class at my feminisation school. One badly-behaved husband, two male employees, a son and a nephew to deal with. A real mixed bag of naughty males to improve. "She looked Patrick over again. "I'll bring my manager over."

Fiona broke away from the group. Patrick scanned the pub with escalating horror. Vulnerability crept up his long slim stockinged legs. A chill whipped around his bottom. Fiona returned with a young woman in a smart black trouser suit who held a white apron in one hand.

"This is Suzie, she's the manager of my pub restaurant. She'll make sure that Patty learns the job and works hard."

Patrick flinched at the words *hard work*. He had never had a real job in his life, unless he counted the two days working at Elizabeth's office. That was more the hard work of humiliation rather than any physical work.

The ladies all kissed each other on the cheeks. Elizabeth and Clara left. Patrick remained standing like a statue, feeling uncomfortable in the short skirt. More customers were arriving, the men's eyes drawn to Patrick's long exposed legs.

"I'll leave Patty with you, Suzie. I have to get to my classes." Fiona left.

Suzie pursed her lips. Her auburn straight hair framed a chalky-white face with blue eyes. "Put this on," she ordered, passing Patrick the white apron.

He fixed in on. It had a frill around the edge and was a couple of inches longer than his little skirt. Suzie shook her head. "Turn round. You don't have a clue. You need a nice big bow at the back."

She tied the bow and patted him playfully on his bottom. "Right, pretty girl, let's get to work. You still look a little masculine under all that femininity, but with that short skirt and those long legs…" She stopped talking and nodded to herself. She placed a finger on her chin and a thin smile appeared. "Our customers are going to *love* you."

End of Part 2

Dear Reader,

I hope you enjoyed the second book in the three-part series 'Petticoated and Pretty'. In book three we'll find out how the feminised and pretty Patrick gets on working in Fiona's gastropub

Please could you spare a moment to share your thoughts on Petticoated and Pretty 2 by posting a quick review.

And don't forget to subscribe to my **newletter.**

Thank you so much for reading my stories,
Lady Alexa
xxx

Printed in Great Britain
by Amazon